About the Author

Born in North Yorkshire, I served a five year engineering apprenticeship and after gaining the appropriate qualifications spent many years teaching engineering. I worked for a number of colleges as a lecturer and many industrial companies as an engineer. I live in West Yorkshire with my wife, Joan, a pharmacist. We have three married children and six grandchildren, who all live in the area.

This is a work of fiction. Names, characters, businesses, places, events and incidents are either the products of the author's imagination or used in a fictitious manner. Any resemblance to actual persons, living or dead, or actual events is purely coincidental.

A COURAGEOUS BREED

B.E. TURNER

A COURAGEOUS BREED

In memory of the many who lived through the horrendous events of the first half of the twentieth century.

Vanguard Press

VANGUARD PAPERBACK

© Copyright 2022
B.E. Turner

The right of B.E. Turner to be identified as author of
this work has been asserted by him in accordance with the
Copyright, Designs and Patents Act 1988.

All Rights Reserved

No reproduction, copy or transmission of this publication
may be made without written permission.
No paragraph of this publication may be reproduced,
copied or transmitted save with the written permission of the
publisher, or in accordance with the provisions
of the Copyright Act 1956 (as amended).

Any person who commits any unauthorised act in relation to
this publication may be liable to criminal
prosecution and civil claims for damages.

A CIP catalogue record for this title is
available from the British Library.

ISBN 978 1 80016 407 9

Vanguard Press is an imprint of
Pegasus Elliot MacKenzie Publishers Ltd.
www.pegasuspublishers.com

First Published in 2022

Vanguard Press
Sheraton House Castle Park
Cambridge England

Printed & Bound in Great Britain

Dedication

In memory of all those who gave up their freedom and in many cases their lives in two world wars. My grandfather Edward Turner who was killed during the battle of Messines in the Great War and my Father Edward who served in the Second World War.

Acknowledgements

I would like to thank the team at Pegasus for all their help in getting this story to print.

Further, I would like to say thank you to my wife, Joan, for putting up with my absence when writing.

Chapter 1
1900

Robert Evans was born on the 1 February 1901 to David and Mary Evans in Mary's family home at Stokesley, North Yorkshire. This event was just after the memorable event, that of Queen Victoria's death at the age of eighty-one years on 22 January 1901.

David Evans was from Llangollen, a small town in South Wales, and had met Mary Hutton in Llandudno while on holiday. Mary was with her mum, dad and sister June; their home was in the Yorkshire town of Stokesley where her dad was the local chemist and ran a prosperous shop. At that time, travel was not very easy although train journeys were becoming more frequent, enabling more families to go on holiday for the first time.

David was a young sergeant in the South Wales Borderers, the 24th Regiment of Foot, and had won a Victoria Cross at the age of eighteen years for his courage during the Anglo — Zulu wars in 1879 at the battle of Rorke's Drift. Mary had trained as a nurse and was now a sister in the local general hospital. They were both twenty-two years old when they had met and fallen in love. The following year, 1891, they were married. A year later, a daughter Emily arrived, followed two years later by another daughter Sarah.

During these years, they had a very happy family life although David was often away on duty; however, the Boer War started on the 11 October 1899. Shortly after this, in June 1900, David's regiment was sent out to South Africa and unfortunately, he was killed at the Battle of Nooitgedacht in December of that year.

Although Robert was born healthy, he was a big baby and his mother had complications from which in those days she did not recover and sadly died. After having two daughters, his father would have been delighted at the birth of a son. The three children were now orphans. Both the grandparents rallied round and decisions were made to look after the children. As it happened, Mary's sister June who had been married in 1899 had given birth to a baby girl called Millicent. June was a wonderful mother and was only too happy to bring up Bobby, as he was called, so with some financial help from Granddad Hutton, Bobby would live with June. In those days, there was no welfare state so it was a good thing most of the families had reasonable jobs. June was married to Bill Thompson, a farmer; he had just taken over running his father's farm, Cherryfields, which was near Hutton Rudby. He was quite willing to have a boy in the farmhouse.

The eldest daughter Emily was to live with the Welsh grandparents. Dr Evans was a GP, he and his wife had a married daughter Gwen who had left home, so they were more than happy to look after one of their son's daughters. Sarah lived with Mary's parents in Stokesley and in time was to become a pharmacist like her granddad.

Cherryfields farm was a mixed farm with a dairy herd, sheep, pigs, hens, ducks and a number of crops. In those days, farming was very labour-intensive so Bill employed five permanent labourers and some casual seasonal staff besides their faithful dogs and horses.

Bobby was loved by June and Bill. He grew up to be a strong little boy who believed they were his mummy and daddy. Bobby thought Milly was his sister, they played together endlessly as toddlers and on a busy farm, it was most helpful to their parents. The two children were of a similar age so they both started in the village school together.

The village school had two buildings, one for children aged five to eight years, the other known as the big school for children nine to fourteen years, and each building had two classrooms. Each classroom had a teacher and the Head Master Mr Brown was in charge of the school. He had fought in the Boar War and was very strict but fair. Most of the children loved him.

Bobby did well at school; although, he was always happier on the farm or out with his pals. Everyone in the village knew each other, the children had friends from the school who also lived in the village.

Bobby and Milly were soon helping out on the farm, first watching as toddlers and helping to collect eggs and feed some of the animals. During these early years, they would occasionally have visits from both of Bobby's grandparents and Bill's mother and father. Sarah and sometimes Emily would come with their grandparents. It was usually at the weekend when the children would play together.

Bobby was a bright little boy and was starting to wonder why they had three grandparents. He knew there was something special about Sarah and Emily and the way they hugged him, there was a loving bond.

On one weekend in 1906, it was Bobby's fifth birthday, everyone arrived at the farm on Saturday. June who was an excellent cook and baker had made a lot of sandwiches, cakes and a scrumptious birthday cake with five candles. They all gathered in the dining room for this special occasion — normally, they ate in the farm kitchen. As usual, they said grace and proceeded to eat and drink tea amidst a hubbub of chatter and laughter.

Bill stood up and said, "It is now time for someone to blow out the candles, I wonder who that is?"

At that, Bobby shouted out, "It's me!"

The cake was lit and placed in front of him and with one or two big breaths, he blew out the candles as all sang happy birthday. Now came an announcement from Grandpa Evans.

"Right," he said, "it is now time to tell you, Bobby, that your father was my son who was killed in the Boar War and your mother was Emily and Sarah's mother who died when you were born."

Bobby was not that surprised; however, he piped up, "Can I still have my mum and dad?"

"Of course, you can," said June and hugged him.

In time, Bobby understood who he was and was very proud to be called Evans and not Thompson at school.

At senior school, Bobby soon made friends with Willy Brown, who lived in the village. His father was the village policeman. They became inseparable as both were similar; they both enjoyed sports and doing PT. Bobby was good at Maths and Science whereas Willy was good at English and History.

An older boy called George Baker who was a bit of a bully kept pushing the younger boys around and demanding sweets from the other pupils. Bobby had got to like Cathy Clark, whose family had moved from Pickering to take over the village shop. It was when George approached Cathy on the playground and was trying to force her to give him her sweets that Bobby got mad. Although George was older than Bobby, he was big for his age. Also, with working on the farm, he was strong and gave George a powerful punch on the chin.

Fortunately for Bobby, the bell rang for them to go into class and all the children lined up with George staggering into his line, holding a sore chin.

George said out loud, "See you in the field."

All the children knew the field at the back of the school where the boys settled their problems with a fight.

After school, Cathy, who also liked Bobby, said to him, "You don't need to fight over me. I will give him some sweets and that should make a truce."

Bobby said, "He's had it coming to him for some time, he needs taking down a peg or two."

So, to shouts of "fight, fight" from some of the other children, most of them wandered over to the field where the two boys met. Bobby was more prepared to fight, he had had some boxing lessons from one of the farm hands who had been a boxer, so they exchanged punches, with George getting some punches in at first. Soon, with shouts of support from many of the children, Bobby had the advantage and with a tremendous right hook felled George, who ended up flat on the ground.

Someone shouted, "You have killed him!", but he came round, got up and admitted defeat. He never bullied anyone again and Bobby had made a name for himself, especially with Cathy.

During these years, Bobby spent a lot of his time helping out on the farm. Bill was a good farmer and a decent man who treated Bobby as a son. Bobby loved the horses; there were the shires Brutus and Clare who did the heavy work like ploughing and two Cleveland Bays Sandy and Pearl who pulled the traps and carts and doubled up for riding. Bobby looked after the horses, cleaned them, fed them and mucked out the stables, he even got a chance to ride them. He helped out when the crops needed harvesting and when lambing took place in the spring.

In the spring of 1906, June gave birth to another girl Sally and a year later, a son Tommy, which was a relief as Bill wanted a son to carry on the family name. The birth of Tommy had been difficult, June was advised to seriously consider not having any more children. At that time, Grandma Hutton and Sarah came to help out; however, Bobby and Milly still had extra jobs to do. An extra job was to help with the milking, they had to see to pouring the milk into churns then take them down to the lane for the diary wagon to collect before they went to school.

Village life went on as it had done for generations. There was a butcher's, a baker's and a general store cum post office which sold groceries and vegetables and a host of other goods a family might need. This was Cathy's home. There was one pub, the Bull, where Bill tried to pop in at least once a week. Sunday was the holy day, all the shops were closed and most people went to church or chapel. Bobby and Cathy's families were Baptists and went to the Baptist chapel. In those days, they went to church in the morning, the children to Sunday school in the afternoon and an evening service was always held. Easter, Whitsuntide, harvest, bonfire, Christmas and Empire Day were all celebrated by most of the villagers. Once a year, most towns and villages had an agricultural show where everyone tried to meet up and have a good time. Bill showed his cattle and horses at the great Yorkshire show in Harrogate, this meant all the family were involved. Bobby looked after the horses which took the cattle to the show, the others followed in the passenger cart.

As Sally and Tommy grew into toddlers, it became easier for Bobby and Milly to get away to meet their friends from school. They often went to meet them on the village green, near Cathy's shop, from where they would set out on walks. Sometimes on a Saturday, they would go further to one of the dales such as Kildale or Commondale and take a picnic. The river Leven ran round the village and at High Leven they could go swimming. Bobby and most of his pals learned to swim in the river.

One day after school, Willy, who collected birds' eggs, said to Bobby, "Come on down to the woods near the river, I want to find an owl's egg."

Milly and Cathy who had become close friends said they would tag along too. Off they went down the lane by the school and through a gate that led into the wood by the river. A path led along, round the village to a bridge that allowed the road from Hutton to Stokesley to pass.

"There that big oak has a nest in it," shouted Cathy.

"Where is it?" Bobby and Willy shouted back in unison.

"There you silly boys," said Milly.

"Oh yes, I can see it now." Then Willy started to climb the tree. It was very high up to the nest.

"Do be careful," said Bobby. "Can you manage?"

"Yes," said Willy, as he reached the nest. Suddenly, an owl flew from the nest to the surprise of the egg thief, and he nearly fell off the branch.

"I've got an egg!" shouted Willy.

"Good!" said Milly. "Now come down before you break your neck."

Willy had just got down when a cry came from the other side of the river, Mrs Brown the baker's wife had been out walking with her two children of five and six. Betsy the little one had fallen in the river which was flowing quite quick.

"She can't swim and neither can I!" said Mrs Brown.

Without hesitation, Bobby threw off his blazer and shoes, dived in and swam towards the struggling child. He got to her and managed to hold her above water as they were taken downstream by the flow. The others rushed after him on paths each side of the river as they headed towards the bridge. Bobby with a great effort swam to a landing area near the bridge, got out of the water with little Betsy and collapsed in a heap. The others arrived to see the rescue. Mrs Brown hugged her child and Bobby alike; she was so grateful and said she would never forget what he had done. Mrs Brown wanted them to come with her back to the shop, but Milly said, "Sorry, we must get home now or my mum will be worried."

They agreed to pop round to the shop after school the next day and have cakes and lemonade.

They all headed home; Cathy to the general store, Willy to the police house and Bobby and Milly to the farm.

"Where have you two been?" said June as they entered the kitchen.

"What on earth have you been up to?" said Bill. "You are soaking, your school uniform is a mess."

After telling their tale, they were forgiven.

"Get upstairs and get your farming clothes on before you get a cold," said June.

Their farming clothes, as they were called, were for working and playing when they got home from school. Once downstairs, they all settled down to the evening meal.

Chapter 2
1914

Mechanisation was being introduced to farming. Although Bill was slow to change, he did buy a Dennis 3-ton lorry which could be used for transporting goods and people. They could get to see Bobby's and Milly's grandparents easier, especially the Welsh side of the family. Granddad Evans as a doctor already had a car for his country rounds; doctors in those days called on their sick patients. His car was an Austin 7 hp. They would stay at the farm in the summer and the children would go and stay with the Evans family and have a welcome holiday in Wales. Granddad Hutton had just bought a Standard Ten and arrived at the farm with Grandma Hutton and Sarah early one Sunday morning to take June and the children to church, the others followed in the lorry. Granddad Hutton was very proud of his car and just had to show it to the rest of the family; after all, he had saved up for years to get one, ever since he had read about the first combustion engine.

At the beginning of the year, Bobby had turned fourteen, then Willy had his fourteenth birthday in May; however, although they could leave school, it was customary to stay on till the summer when the whole class finished school. Some children could stay on at high school in Stokesley but not the boys, they were ready to work. During these months, as the boys were quite big for their age, their families started to call them Bob and Will, which seemed more appropriate.

The younger of the children on the farm, Sally and Tommy, were at the same school as Bob and Milly. They all got on well. Bob, being one of the big boys in the school and respected, made sure they were all right. Mr Brown the head master said Bob was a born leader and thanked him for helping to stop any bullying, making the school a happy place for all the children. Sally and Tommy had their little jobs to do on the farm. Soon, they were taking over from the older children, which meant Bob could devote more time to the other tasks, such as helping with the milking and, of course, the horses before school. Milly was now spending more time helping June in the house learning to cook and mend although she still helped with the pigs and hens.

One morning at breakfast, June started in alarm. "Tommy, are you all right?"

He was flushed and not looking well, they all looked at him.

"I am not feeling well," he said.

"Right," said Bill, "let's have a look at your chest," and sure enough, he was covered in spots.

"It's measles," said June, "we will have to call the doctor. Get back up to bed."

"Let's have a look at the rest of you, these things go round. We must inform the school," said Bill.

The others seemed OK and were told to keep away from Tommy. Bob was instructed to tell the doctor and the headmaster so the other children could be checked as measles could be deadly. Doctor Good arrived at the farm within the hour and confirmed it was measles, he gave June some medicine to help lower Tommy's temperature and cream to put on the spots. It was not until around 1950 that the first measles vaccine was available so for a few days, it was touch-and-go for little Tommy who was quite ill. The family were all very worried as news arrived that some children in the area had died of the dreaded disease.

After five days, Tommy started to recover. He had a strong constitution, he would one day join the parachute regiment and fight for his country at Arnhem in the Second World War.

On the seventh day, Tommy came down to breakfast saying, "Can I go back to school now? I feel OK."

June told him he should wait a few days to put some weight back on and build up his strength.

None of the other children in the family had contracted the measles, further the school was also clear after the warning had been given and several children had been kept at home to recover or not, as was the case.

Bob and Cathy had become close friends, as had Milly and Will. They all went to school and church youth club together. They sometimes would now go out in pairs instead of a group, although with strict time limits.

One Saturday morning, Bob asked Bill, "Can I bring Cathy round to show her how to ride?"

"Why, of course, you can," said Bill, "but make sure she's safe, take things easy at first till she's confident."

The others had a sly giggle at Bob bringing his girlfriend home. June told them not to be silly.

Bill had his truck now so the Cleveland Bays were often ridden by the family, although on occasions they still pulled the carts on market days, on Sundays and when the Dennis had to be serviced or repaired.

Bob met Cathy on the village green near the shop.

"Come on," he said. "I have a surprise for you, we are off to the farm."

"I hope it's a good one," replied Cathy.

They were soon at the farm on the outskirts of the village. "Right, now wait a minute," said Bob as he popped into the farmhouse and came out with a scarf. "Now put this on."

Cathy allowed him to lead her by the hand blindfolded to the stables where Sandy and Pearl were already saddled up and ready to go.

"Now let's take off the scarf," and to Cathy's surprise, she saw the waiting horses. "Would you like to go riding?" asked Bob.

"Would I?" said Cathy. "I always wished I could ride."

"So you shall. Come on, let's get you on Pearl."

So, after a few steady lessons, Cathy who seemed at home on a horse was soon an accomplished horse woman. The two of them often went riding together over the fields and moors of North Yorkshire.

One sad event occurred in early June. Cathy's dad had a stroke and unfortunately did not recover. Mr Clark had been injured in the Boar War in the head and chest. He had been fine since before Cathy was born, but the doctor said the head injury could have contributed to his stroke. Most of the villagers had grown to like Mr Clark as a cheerful, happy person when serving them in the shop so there was a big turn-out at his funeral. Bob's family had become very close to the Clarks. June helped Brenda with the reception and Bob felt very sorry for them as Cathy was the only child. He promised to help if any heavy lifting was required.

In July, the school term was over, it was the end of school for most of the children of Bob's age. A party had been arranged, and each child was asked to bring something to eat and the teachers got together to get some soft drinks like lemonade and dandelion and burdock. What a time they had! One lad played the accordion while the rest danced and sang some of the old songs like "Down at the Old Bull and Bush" and "On Ilkley Moor Bar T'at".

Bob walked Cathy home after the party. When they got under the big tree outside the shop, they looked into each other's eyes and could not resist their first kiss and cuddle. Both realised their lives would be different now; Cathy would have to work in the shop and Bob would work at the farm. They still met up with their friends, Bob played football and cricket on the local sports ground and Cathy played netball.

On 4 August, after an ultimatum given to Germany to withdraw from Belgium was refused, it was announced by the Prime Minister Lloyd George that Britain was at war and so began World War I.

During the next few months, many of the older boys and men of the village and of the country as a whole were to head to France with the expectation that it would be all over by Christmas. Bob and Will were eager to go and fight the Germans before it was all over; however, they were too young and so they were disappointed.

June said, "It's just as well, going out to a strange country at your age is not right."

Life on the farm had to go on, people needed food and animals had to be looked after. It was one of the best summers that anyone could remember that led to a bumper harvest. Bob worked hard helping Bill, but his heart told him he should be helping his country. It was always the topic of conversation when he met up with Cathy, Will and other friends in the village.

16 December turned out to be a nice morning. Bob and Cathy decided to go for a ride over the moors to Westerdale. It was around eight o'clock as they reached the moors when Bob said to Cathy, "I can hear loud bangs in the distance, can you?"

"Yes," said Cathy, "it seems to be towards the coast."

They rode further on, heading east, when suddenly, they heard a strange whining noise, and in the distance, a massive explosion on the moors. Cathy was alarmed.

"Let's go back!" she said.

"Yes," Bob remarked. "We need to know what the hell is going on!"

On their arrival at the farm, news had spread; it was a German raid. They could hear the noise from the farm, it was very unsettling and as they found out later, a bombardment by the German fleet was taking place along the North east coast. People thought it was a precursor to an invasion, Bill and Bob said they would fight them on the beaches if they came. Even little

Tommy and the girls said they would fight. June said, "Not till you all get older."

Scarborough, Whitby, Hartlepool and other towns on the coast got a hammering from the German battleships the *Derfflinger* and the *Von der Tann*. They fired 500 shells at Scarborough alone, from a SK L/50 navel gun which fired shells 30.5cm in diameter causing substantial damage. It was later found that the reason for the bombardment was to humiliate the Royal Navy, then the mightiest navy in the world, and intimidate the public. It did not work; in fact, it caused the opposite effect. The German ships were able to accomplish this due to the fact that some of the Royal navy ships had been sent to the South Atlantic, other ships were not near at the time but soon caught up with them.

The raid caused belligerent fury among the population. When the notices were posted in the village saying your country needs you, remember Scarborough, the recruitment escalated considerably. All the young lads were dying to join up, especially Bob and Will; however, they were too young to go. Many did go as the war on the continent raged on.

Bill was all but resolved to go, but as a farmer he was more needed at home. June was relieved that none of them were to be involved.

Christmas came, the war still continued on with reports of a number of men from the village either gone missing or killed in action. All the family agreed to come to the farm on Christmas day. June invited Cathy and her mum and Bob's sisters arrived, Emily in her new uniform. They all went to chapel in the morning to celebrate the birth of Jesus Christ. Then, what a time they had! It was a good job the farm had a good-sized dining room, they all just about managed to get round the table. The youngest children sat at a side table. Bill made a toast wishing everyone well in the coming year.

After the meal, the younger ones played games such as snakes and ladders and pass the parcel, the adults cleared up and sat talking of better times. Bobs sisters parted with a tinge of sadness as Emily would soon be going overseas. They all said their farewells with hugs and kisses. Bob saw Cathy and her mum home to the shop.

Chapter 3
1915

Llangollen is a beautiful small town on the River Dee in Denbighshire. This is where Dr Evans, Bob's granddad, his father's dad, had his practice and was a consultant at the local hospital. Emily, like her father before, had grown up there and had been very happy. She had been able to go to the private Grammar school and had done well at her studies.

Her granddad had wanted her to become a doctor; however, at sixteen years old, she said, "I want to be a nurse like my mother."

Her grandma said, "If that's what you want to do, love, then do it as I did."

Her grandparents had met at a hospital in Cardiff where they were both working at the time. She left school and started nursing at the local community hospital. It was hard work but she loved it, she was a bright girl and was soon to qualify as a staff nurse. During her time as a young nurse, she met and became close friends with two other nurses; Dolly Jones and Pat Reeves. In the spare time they had, a trip to the local dance or walks in the wonderful countryside was a welcome change from the hospital. They did go out with local young men, but it soon became apparent they would have to go out on their own, as a lot of the men were joining the forces.

It was nearing the end of 1914 when Emily announced to her friends, "I have thought long and hard about this, but feel it is my duty to help the boys who are laying down their lives for us and their country. I am joining the army."

"Are you sure?" said Dolly. "It means going to the front."

"I have been thinking the same thing," said Pat.

"I am not staying here on my own," said Dolly. "Shall we all join up together?"

Although their parents and grandparents were not too happy with the decision, but they were also proud of them. After all, the girls were all over twenty-one so it was up to them.

An application was made and within a few weeks, they were accepted. They were short of qualified nurses and were enlisted into Queen Alexandra's imperial military nursing service. They reported for training on battlefield techniques, where they received their uniform and necessary kit. By Christmas, they were told they would be joining an army division in the new year.

The girls went home to Llangollen where they were able to celebrate Christmas and New Year. Emily and her grandparents travelled to see Bob, Sarah and the rest of the family in Yorkshire, before spending the New Year in Wales with the Welsh side of the family.

By mid-January, they were told to report to the East Lancashire Regiment barracks near Preston and join the 87th (1st West Lancs) field ambulance under the command of the Royal Army Medical Corps. They were to be attached to the 29th Army division, who became known as the 'Incomparable Division'.

After meeting up with the other nurses, they were introduced to the doctors and orderlies who made up the field ambulance. With some effort, the girls were able to get a room together. No one knew where they were heading. Emily had been told by one of the doctors that he thought they were to embark from Plymouth in a few days' time. She passed the information on to Dolly and Pat, who said, "At last, we will be doing something useful."

However, they were transported to an army hospital outside Plymouth where they were to wait and help out for a few weeks while a fleet was being assembled. This was their first taste of the terrible results of warfare, the nurses were kept busy helping out with the wounded returning from the western front.

One evening in early April, they were told they were to embark aboard a hospital ship the next morning, the whole division was to be landed at Cape Helles near Gallipoli where the ANZACS had landed. The idea was to isolate the Turks from Europe and Germany and hence help end the war. Further, it was hoped it would draw Bulgaria and Greece into the war on the allied side.

During the long voyage, the nurses were to refrain from fraternising with the males on board but for someone like Emily it was impossible, she had become friendly with one of the doctors called Edward Mills, Ted for short. They had seen each other a few times in Plymouth. She a pretty nurse and he a handsome young doctor, it was love at first sight. They found they had a lot in common such as their love of medicine and of the countryside. His home was in Nantwich, a small town in Cheshire. They agreed it was wise not to get too involved, they would be friends. Dolly and Pat said she should be careful as the matron would not be pleased if she found out.

The first task of the division was to capture the forts that guarded the straits of the Dardanelles. Both French and British troops were involved in the landings on 25 April 1915. After a bombardment from the battleships in the fleet, the troops of the Hampshire Regiment and the Munster and Dublin Fusiliers made the first landings from the troop carriers; however, they ran into fierce resistance from the Ottoman army resulting in many casualties.

The Lancashire fusiliers were then landed further round the bay and counter-attacked, making a flanking movement. They fought bravely and due to their effort, a bridgehead was formed. The regiment was awarded six VCs in the action. Thus, the other troops were able to land with the field ambulance of the Royal Army Medical Corps.

Emily, Dolly and Pat were all made ward sisters, each having responsibility for running a ward, which meant not only treating patients but seeing supplies and equipment were available. Emily was often called upon to assist in operating theatre working with Dr Mills, they became a rapid response team. The work was exhausting and dangerous, most of the nurses worked twelve hours a day non-stop, with the noise of battle and risk of a stray bullet or exploding shell ever present. The wounds of the boys were terrible, some of them were very young. Many did not recover and often died being comforted by a young nurse.

Nurses were not immune from injury. When some of the nurses were hanging out their washing, a shell burst nearby, showering them with shrapnel. Unfortunately, Pat was wounded badly. She was rushed into the operating theatre where Emily and Ted did their best to save her but she died of her wounds. This was a blow to Emily and Dolly who had lost a close friend from home in Wales. It was very sad for Emily as she was asked to write a letter to inform Pat's family of their bereavement.

After this event, with two nurses losing their lives and a number with injuries, the unit was moved to a safer location.

Chapter 4
1916

In January 1916, a decision was made to evacuate the 29th Army division back to England to regroup. They had fought well against overwhelming odds and to save more men to fight in France, it was necessary to get them home. Further, there was no chance of sending reinforcements. There had been thirty-four thousand casualties and twelve VCs were won by the division; they had done their duty. Under the cover of shelling from the fleets of battleships, the remaining fit soldiers boarded their troop ships, the medics and wounded were taken aboard the hospital ship. There was no resistance once at sea, so after a rough passage they got back safely to Portsmouth.

Bob had worked hard at the farm, in fact, all the family had more jobs to do in aid of the war effort. Some of the men who had worked for Bill had now gone to fight. Bob often helped Cathy in the shop with heavy lifting, they were now very much in love but at sixteen years old, they did not want to get too serious. One thing they missed was riding as unfortunately, the two Cleveland Bays had been requisitioned by the army and sent to France. The family at the farm had to use the heavy horses or the truck.

Bob and little Tommy, who was nine now, got on well together. They often played football with Will and a few other boys on the school sports field. The nearest league team was at Middlesbrough.

One Saturday, a group of them which included Cathy and Milly arranged to go to see an FA cup game at the Ayresome Park ground. A single-decker bus ran between the villages and the big towns on Teesside and because of its many stops took ages to travel what was a fairly short distance. It was 3 May and because of the rain the night before, a shroud of mist was hanging over the moors.

As they headed towards Danby, Will shouted out, "Look in the sky!"

As they all looked, a massive shape like a big fat sausage appeared out of the mist.

"What is it?" Cathy remarked.

"It's one of those German Zeppelins, I've read about them," said Bob. Suddenly, there was tremendous explosions as the German's dropped bombs over Danby High Moor. They had mistaken Danby for the industrial town of Stockton-on-Tees. A number of Zeppelins had been on a raid to hit the iron works at Skinningrove and Carlin How and then to head for Stockton and Middlesbrough, it was later termed 'Britain's First

Blitz'. The idea again was to demoralise the population and destroy vital industries.

One of the Zeppelins dropped a bomb on a farm as the bus was passing and then passed over them. They were very scared but then relieved as it went towards Rosedale Abbey. The farm was ablaze.

The driver stopped the bus and said, "Some of you older boys, come with me, let's see if we can help."

Bob, Will and two other lads headed over to the farm. What a sight, they found the barn on fire; however, the house had been missed. One farm hand was injured, another dead. They all helped to put the blaze out. The driver of the bus said he would stop at the next village to phone the emergency services, so they all got on board the bus. He was not to head for Danby as the place was ablaze, so he told his passengers that the best thing was to get them home. They stopped at Castleton and he informed the police to send help to the farm on the moors.

On their return, Bob and his friends were relieved to see the Stokesley and Hutton Rudby area had not been hit.

When they got off the bus at home, Bob was very angry at what he had seen and said to Will, "The next time they come recruiting, I am ready to enlist."

Will agreed to go with him. Cathy and Milly said they were concerned and told them, "You must be eighteen to enlist so you will have to wait."

Soon, movements were afoot to enlist more men, the Germans had pushed forward towards the Somme and a big offensive was being planned. The recruiting teams were going round in every county with instructions to enlist as many men as they could. When two strapping lads turned up looking for all the world like eighteen-year-olds, they were enlisted without question. Cathy saw they had enlisted and went to the police house and the farm to tell them the news. Bill and June were concerned and dashed to the village centre. Too late, they had signed up and had to report for duty the next day at eight when they would be picked up by an army truck from the Yorkshire Regiment (later to be called the Green Howards).

On their return to Portsmouth, the 29th division were given a few days' leave, then they had to return to regroup before being sent to France. Dr Ted Mills, or Captain Mills as he was now called after his work at Cape Helles, was very much in love with Emily who had also been promoted to a matron. She felt the same way, so when Ted suggested they have a break in London, she jumped at the chance. Ted's family had a flat in London, his father was an MP who was at home in Nantwich which meant the flat was free.

They set off early on a Friday morning to be back for Monday. The London South Western Steam Railway (LSWR) ran from Portsmouth to London

Waterloo station. Travelling first-class, they really enjoyed the journey. Ted said he was to spare no expense for their future was uncertain. On arrival in London, they headed for the flat which was not far from the strand. Although it looked small from the outside, the facilities inside were more than adequate. Emily said it was delightful and headed for the bedroom with her suitcase. Ted followed her with his suitcase, put it down and looked into her eyes; that was enough. They kissed and he held her in a passionate embrace. They soon removed their clothes and fell onto the bed.

It was the first time for them both. With gentle care for each other, they both responded to their love making with urgency and passion. Later, they managed to make a meal in the flat. It was then that Ted said, "I want to marry you, will you have me?"

"I love you," said Emily, "but it would be unwise until the war is over."

"We could get married while we are in London," Ted replied.

"No, I want a proper wedding so can we wait?"

"Right," said Ted. "In that case, we'll make a promise to marry and tomorrow I will buy you a ring."

Next morning, after a night of passion, Ted took Emily to Mayfair where the Royal Jewellers Garrards had their premises, 24 Albemarle Street. Emily said it was too expensive; however, Ted insisted so she picked out a solitaire diamond gold ring.

They had a lovely day first visiting the London Museum then on to Piccadilly by underground to visit the National Gallery; what a treat for Emily who had never been to London! The day was finished with a meal at Simpsons in the Strand, followed by taking in a show at the Hackney Empire to see *Follow the Crowd*. On Sunday, they went to a service in St Paul's cathedral followed by a trip on the river Thames before returning to the flat for their return journey to Portsmouth. Ted and Emily had to return to their billets. Dolly was the first to notice the ring, but soon, all the staff of their field ambulance knew they were a couple. Within six weeks, the whole division now supplemented by extra men and in some cases new regiments were embarking for France to head for the Somme.

Bob and Will said their farewells to family and friends who had managed to see them off from the village green. They were transported in trucks, picking up other men and boys at other villages and towns on the way. On arrival at Richmond Barracks, they were marched to a large store building where they were kitted out with uniforms, given their platoon number, told to change into their uniforms and shown to their billets. Each man had a bunk bed and a locker. Bob and Will managed to stay next to each other, and the lads in their billet were of a similar age, most from North or East Yorkshire.

Training normally took three months; however, they were given two months of extensive combat familiarisation, twelve to fourteen hours a day. This consisted of PT, drill, weapon training and assault course trials with route marches to get them ready. At the end of the training supervised by Platoon Sergeant Sid Timpson, they had become a coherent fighting force. Bob and Will had both gained weight and although the food was quite good, it was muscle not fat they had acquired. It was at this point a decision was made to appoint section leaders; Bob had shown he was a natural leader and was well-liked by the lads in his billet, so he became Corporal Evans and Will Lance Corporal Brown. There were four sections in a platoon, each section had twelve men led by a corporal. A Lieutenant James Kennedy led the platoon with Sergeant Timpson. The sections competed with each other to be the best. Bob's section often won, this enhanced their training and was taken well by the men as it won them the Platoon Award. Bob had got to know his own section well and he and Will had become pals with two of the lads, Gordon James from Barnard Castle and Peter Granger from Stockton-on-Tees. At last, after two months, they were given leave for the weekend and told to return on the Sunday evening. They were heading for France first thing Monday morning.

Bob and Will got a train to Stockton from Richmond and then a bus to Hutton, arriving just before lunch. As they got off the bus, people greeted them wishing them well and then Cathy and Milly who had been working in the shop dashed over and embraced them.

Cathy said, "How happy we are to see you." Then, after sometime telling them what they had been up to, all agreed to meet up later. Bob and Will went to see their parents, what a welcome Bob received from Bill, June and the children. At lunch, Bob realised he had missed June's home cooking and said, "The food at the barracks was OK but not a patch on yours, Mum."

"Come on then," said Bill, "tell us what you have done to get two stripes," and so they heard the story and how they were off to France.

After lunch, Tommy and Sally took Bob round the farm to see the animals and crops, some of which Bob had planted earlier in the year. He helped with the horses and chattered with the old farm hands before having a game of football with Tommy. After dinner, Bob went into the village with Milly to meet Cathy and Will. They had a walk round by the river and after a kiss and cuddle on the river bank, made their way to the village pub, The Kings Head. It was a warm night so they were able to sit outside and enjoy a shandy.

On Sunday morning, the families gathered at the chapel for the service. Every one wished Bob and Will good luck and a safe return. After lunch at the farm, Bob had to get back to the village to see Cathy and meet Will before their trip back on the bus and train to Richmond.

At the barracks, they had to prepare for moving out in the morning. Six platoons were to reinforce a battalion at the front. They met up with Gordon and Peter who said some of the lads were afraid of going, but at the same time eager to be on the move. Bob said to his section, "Look, lads, we are all in this together. Just do your best for your country and your mates and if you were not afraid, I would be a little worried, so get a good night's sleep while you have a bed to sleep in."

Early on Monday, the 300 men, most of them under twenty years old, were led by a Captain Roger Grey. They marched into Richmond to the rail station where a special train was waiting to take them to the troop ship in Portsmouth. On arrival, provision had been made for them to stay in a naval barracks until their ship was ready to sail. For three days, they continued training so as to be ready for action, each of the last two evening's half the men from the contingent were allowed to have a break in town. Bob and his pals went into town and ended up in the Black Bull where a number of other Yorkshire lads, sailors and lads from other regiments were drinking. It was good to listen to a little band playing and drinking. Bob had his first pint of beer, he usually had shandy, but enjoyed his drink, as did his pals. Suddenly, the peace was shattered; a fight broke out between some Yorkshire lads and some sailors. One had insulted Yorkshire as being a crap place. He probably had never been anywhere near Yorkshire and was drunk. However, things were getting bad as more joined in the fray. Bob saw it was wrong and ordered some lads from his section to come away out, so with Will, Gordon and Peter, he got his lads out just in time before the Military Police arrived.

Next morning, with full pack they boarded the troop ship bound for Le Havre. The journey took five hours. On arrival, they had a meal at a holding station and then travelled by truck to a relief area near Albert to link up with the rest of the Yorkshire battalion.

A big push was planned to force the Germans back and hopefully get them to surrender, so troops were arriving in their thousands from French, British and commonwealth armies. An artillery bombardment started at seven thirty a.m. on 1 July, it was expected to decimate the German defences.

The Yorkshire regiment was dug in between Albert and Gommecourt, Bob and his platoon were directed to the trenches after a march from the relief area. After settling in, they managed to get some sleep before being woken up by a barrage that lasted several hours.

"What the hell!" said Peter. "Will it never stop?"

They all held their hands to their ears this was their first taste of war. Sergeant Timpson arrived with Lieutenant Kennedy.

"Right, lads," shouted the sergeant, "fix bayonets, we are going over the top so best of luck. This is your chance to show your worth."

With whistles and shouts, the troops on several fronts left their trenches and charged towards the German lines. Halfway across no man's land, the Germans opened fire, they had been in deep bunkers and were little affected by the shells. The platoon reached the German trench and after a bloody battle of hand-to-hand fighting, held it for other troops to move up. The cost was unbelievable; half the platoon was dead or injured, including Gordon. It was sad for Bob and his friends but at least they had survived.

The first battle of the Somme raged back and forward for four months. There were 57,470 casualties of which 19,240 men were killed in action. The Yorkshire Regiment had played a vital part at a great loss. Before they were withdrawn for a rest, Bob's platoon had made another charge forward. Unfortunately, Bob's section, were caught in a shell burst and Bob and Will were both hit with shrapnel. The others were killed. Peter who was unhurt helped them to get back to their trench. Their wounds though not severe were enough to put them out of action. They were taken to a field ambulance behind the lines where they were to receive treatment. The shrapnel had to be removed and the wounds dressed. A nurse came over to assess Bob's wounds, and what a surprise they both got! It was his older sister Emily.

"Bob, what are you doing in this hell hole? You should not be here at your age!" Then she saw Will.

"You too, I don't know." Then she went and kissed them both. "No time for explanations, let's get you seen to."

Then, she gave instructions to get them wheeled in to see the doctor. After their treatment, Emily had a chat with them and they told her how they had come to be at the Somme and how things were when they had left home. Emily told her story and introduced them to her fiancé, Ted. Bob liked him and wished them well.

The next day, they were sent back to England to recover from their wounds. On their arrival, they were sent to a hospital at Catterick. It was two months before they were allowed a short visit home before returning to the Regimental Headquarters in Richmond. The war raged on, men were needed at the front to stop the Germans' advance at all points along the battle lines of the western front.

Chapter 5
1917

Sarah had been brought up with Gran and Granddad Hutton. She was a lively bright girl with blonde hair and lovely blue eyes. She loved her life in Stokesley, a quiet market town set in the stunning Cleveland hills. Sarah often saw her brother Bob at the farm where at holiday times, Emily would come to stay. In those days, the children would all have happy times together. At school, Sarah did well and was good at most subjects; she especially found science and maths of great interest. She helped in the chemist shop where she gained an interest in pharmacy, which her granddad encouraged.

Sarah said to him one day when she was sixteen, "I want to be a pharmacist like you, Granddad."

He said he would help her to achieve her dream. Her friends at school and even some of the teachers told her she would never do it, as at that time very few women entered the scientific professions. That was like a red rag to a bull; Sarah was determined and worked hard to get a good school certificate and applied, with encouragement from her granddad, to University College of London School of Pharmacy.

Sarah was one of the first women to apply to enter the college. She had to go down to London to face an interview panel. Fortunately, the knowledge she had gained in the shop put her in good stead. When asked questions about the relevant drugs and treatments, she could give the correct answers. Some of the questions were not given to the male candidates as Sarah found out later. At home the following week, Sarah received a letter saying the School of Pharmacy had accepted her as an undergraduate student.

With financial help from her grandparents, Sarah was able to stay in London and attend lectures at the university. She managed to share a flat with the only other woman student Joan Goodman who was from Eastbourne. They became close friends, often visiting places of interest at the weekends. It was on one such visit to the London Museum in their final year that the girls met up with Emily and Ted.

"Well, I never!" said Sarah. "Look over there, it's my sister. Emily!" she shouted and they came over, surprised but over-joyed at meeting.

Emily introduced her new fiancé and Sarah introduced her friend. Sarah knew Emily was a nurse working with the army, but did not expect to see her in London.

Ted said, "Come on, let's have a drink together."

In a coffee house just outside the museum, they talked about the war, the girls about their studies and their homes and family. They parted wishing each other well and Emily wished the girls good luck in their exams. During this time, Sarah had met an engineering student called James Whitehead and after several meetings at the local tennis club where they played as partners, he asked her out to dinner. He was from Whitby so they had a lot in common and got on well together.

For the next few months, Sarah worked hard swotting for her finals, then came the exams, in both practical and theoretical pharmacy, which she passed with honours. It was time to make decisions for their futures; Sarah was to return home to help her granddad in the shop, while Joan was to take up a job with a manufacturing company near her home and James was called into service with the Royal Navy. They went out together on the last evening with a number of friends, not knowing if they would see each other again.

James, or Jim as his friends called him, took Sarah for a walk along the embankment where they sat on a bench. It was then he said to Sarah, "I love you, darling."

She responded with "I love you too" and they kissed and cuddled.

Jim and Sarah agreed to write to each other and he would come and see her on his return from the sea. He walked her home to the flat where they had a sad parting.

The next day, Sunday, after saying farewell, Sarah and Joan parted to head to their home towns. It was a long journey by train, first to York and then on to Stokesley where the Huttons picked her up in the car. What a welcome she had at home; Bill, June, the children and Cathy and her mum were all there to welcome her and they had a wholesome tea with June and Grandma's home baking.

Sarah settled in to help in the shop and for a long time was happy. She missed Jim and was always eager to receive his letters and reply. He was now a Junior Engineer Officer aboard a RN Destroyer. Always at the back of her mind was the thought that she should be helping with the war effort like her sister and brother. During this time, she was taught to drive by Granddad Hutton and loved driving. She often took the car out to the farm to see her Aunty June and took the children out for picnics.

One morning, she saw in the local paper they were asking for women to join the new Women's Auxiliary Army Corps, the WAACs as they were called. The corps was being formed because of a need to release men from non-combat duties so they could join the fighting men. She said to her grandparents she felt a need to help and with their reluctant blessing, she applied at the recruiting office in Northallerton. After her interview, she was sent to Aldershot to train as a junior officer.

The training was similar in some ways to the normal army training but not in combat readiness; otherwise, as a junior officer, Sarah had to pass out in the same way as a private, then in extra studies such as understanding management, logistics and battlefield studies. After the first few weeks, their uniforms arrived. Sarah became 1st Lieutenant Evans. When her initial four months' training was finished, she was put in charge of a transport platoon. Drivers were in demand so all her girls could either drive or were taught to drive the army trucks.

It took some time to ensure all the girls were competent. The platoon sergeant was Barbara Jones who was a great help to Sarah and became a close colleague and friend. Barbara had a home in a little village called Corwen in North Wales not more than a few miles from Llangollen, so they had a few things in common. Sarah told Barbara about her father and her family. Barbara who was soon called Babs had been brought up on a farm.

Soon, their time at Aldershot was over; they were told to prepare to go overseas to Belgium. The army on the Belgium salient was to make a great push against the German forces. Their job was to transport troops from the ports to the front to reinforce the divisions of the Yorkshire Regiment and the Welsh Regiment. After which, they would transport supplies and armaments. The first contingent of WAACs was shipped from

Dover to Ostend where Sarah's platoon was given command of their trucks to carry their comrades to positions behind the lines where they would take over from the men. They then were required to head back and forward from the ports to positions at the front with troops arriving from England. It was very hazardous at times.

Sarah and Babs were in the lead truck when Sarah said, "Can you see something in the sky?"

Babs replied, "It's probably one of our aircraft making a reconnoitre of the trenches."

To their surprise, it was flying towards their line of trucks; it had been fairly quiet so they never expected an attack from the sky. Babs pulled the lead truck into the verge while Sarah signalled to the others to get out and scatter. The German plane dropped a couple of bombs, one of which hit and disabled one of the trucks. Some of the soldiers were slightly injured but no one seriously hurt thanks to the girls' quick thinking. To cheers from all at the scene, the German plane was attacked by planes from the Royal Flying Corps and shot down. They had no more problems and were able to get the wounded into the other trucks and transported them to the field ambulance. The other troops were taken to their drop-off points.

This to the mostly young women of the WAACs was a rude awakening to the horrors of war, although it did not deter them but reinforced their determination to do their duty and help the lads at the front. After the bulk of the troops, armaments and supplies had been delivered, Sarah's platoon was allowed a respite; they had been working twelve-to-fourteen-hour days for over a month. They were given leave in Ypres, a town in Flanders. The town had been shelled mercilessly by the Germans; however, some bars and cafés were open and they received a warm welcome.

Sarah and Babs managed to get a warm bed for the night.

Sarah said, "This is heaven after sleeping in our trucks."

Babs agreed so they settled in to enjoy their stay.

Their leave was cut short; after three days, they were told a great push forward was to be made and they would be required to drive ambulances with wounded from the front line. After reaching the holding station, they were told to make ready.

Bob and Will were now fit and well, so after some combat training with a section of new recruits, they were sent back to fight again. During Bob and Will's recovery, the Yorkshire Regiment had been moved to strengthen the division in Flanders. Many other regiments had been sent to a line of defence called the Ypres Salient where trench warfare raged backwards and forwards for years. In an effort to make some gains and push the Germans back, hopefully for good, units of miners from both the British and Commonwealth countries such as the Australians and Canadians had been at work. Both sides had been mining under the enemy trenches to plant explosives and hence gain some advantage. The British plan was to remove the Germans from a dominant position south of Ypres at Messines Ridge and by June 1917, twenty-one mines had been filled with nearly one million pounds of explosives.

Bob and Will, with other men from a number of regiments, arrived at Ostend with full kit, ready to be transported to the holding stations. Although Bob knew his sister Sarah had joined the WAACs, he did not know she was in one of the trucks he had alighted from.

What a sight awaited them; all around were shell holes, broken trees and broken bodies. It was a wilderness of slime pits and corruption, a hell on earth.

Bob's contingent of reinforcements of Yorkshire lads were marched to their positions in the frontline trenches. Bob and Will were welcomed with cheers from the lads of their old platoon. Some of the new lads joined their section to make up the numbers, as the original members had been killed at the Somme. So, Bob was to lead his new section into the next battle.

The third battle of Ypres called the Battle of Messines took place on 7 July 1917. At three ten a.m., nineteen of the twenty-one mines were detonated, which took the Germans by surprise. The Yorkshire infantry advanced over the far edge of the southern ridge with little resistance; however, as they approached Hill 60, the German artillery and machine guns east of the ridge opened fire. The British artillery was less able to suppress them.

At Battle Wood, Bob's platoon was pinned down by machinegun fire and many men were wounded or killed. Seeing a number of his men down, including Will, Bob made a courageous attack single-handedly. He managed to put out the nearest machine gun with hand grenades and proceeded to carry Will back to the nearest trench under fire. He then returned again to collect Captain Kennedy and, although wounded himself, a third time to collect a young lad from his section. His bravery saved three lives and spurred the regiment on to take Battle Wood.

The battle was a victory for the allies that many said was the beginning of the end for the German aggressor.

In Flanders Fields, many men were killed or wounded. The Menin Gate Memorial in Ypres is dedicated to the sixty thousand British and Commonwealth soldiers who have no known graves.

During the battle, Sergeant Timpson had been killed with many others; however, the casualties were less than expected. Later, Bob would be awarded the Distinguished Conduct Medal or DCM and promoted to sergeant. His wounds were not serious, the bullets had grazed him in the arm and leg. All the wounded were sent to the field dressing station. Will had a bad wound in his thigh, the captain a stomach wound and the young soldier a shoulder wound.

All wounds were cleaned and emergency treatment was given, they would then be transported by field ambulance to the nearest port to be sent to a hospital in England. Bob's wounds were not serious enough for a return to home soil so he was to be taken to a recuperation area established behind the lines. As they waited for the ambulances to pick up the wounded, Bob wrote a letter to give to Will to take home to Cathy with instructions to let his family know he was all right.

Will was glad to be going home. He said to Bob, "I wish you could come with me and get away from this hell of a place."

Bob said, "I am a survivor, and in any case, I have to lead the platoon now."

When the ambulances arrived, Bob saw Will and his other wounded friends off, feeling a little sad and very tired. Another ambulance or converted truck for the walking wounded stopped near the field ambulance station and to Bob's surprise, a WAAC officer got out with instructions to collect Bob and other soldiers like him. It was his sister Sarah.

He strolled over and said, "Hello, is it sir or madam I should call you?"

"Bob, is it really you?" She kissed and hugged him and said how wonderful it was to see him. "Get up in the front with me so we can talk on the way."

They helped the other wounded to get into the trucks and with Babs driving the lead truck, they set off away from danger.

Sarah and Bob had a good time exchanging news about the family. She promised to come and see him at the recuperation area if she could. Bob said he would like that, saying nothing about his exploits, only that he caught a couple of grazers and should be healed soon. They arrived at a large house that had been requisitioned by the army for recovery of the wounded, they said they needed them back as quickly as possible. The house was just south of Ypres, set in its own grounds, and with a nursing staff to care for them, it was heaven compared with the trenches.

Bob said goodbye to Sarah and was led into a room with a number of beds in, given pyjamas and helped into bed. His wounds were treated, they gave him some decent food, he then slept for a good twelve hours. After the first two days, Bob was able to get up and get dressed. He visited and talked with the other soldiers and even found time to write some more letters home. Within a fortnight, he was back to full health, when he was told he would soon go back to his unit.

Sarah had some leave so she could visit her brother. She managed to borrow a staff car for a day, drove to the house and picked up Bob. They drove to the medieval town of Bruges and visited the old town with its canals and historic buildings. They enjoyed their day out together with the chance to have a nice meal and drinks at a good restaurant.

"This is a lovely place," said Sarah. "I must remember to bring Jim here after the war."

"It's a nice idea," Bob replied, "that's if you can afford it."

"Yes, that's true, but I can always hope for better times," said Sarah.

On their return to the house, Bob and Sarah parted with a kiss and cuddle as Sarah dropped Bob off on the front drive. Bob didn't stop the talk and jokes from his other bed fellows who thought he was lucky to have an attractive WAAC officer for a sweetheart; little did they know he loved the idea.

The following day, Bob and a number of his other comrades were picked up and taken back to their units. Bob was now in charge of the platoon until another officer could replace the now-promoted Captain Kennedy, who had been in charge of the platoon. Things had gone quiet after the recent battle, with both sides planning their next move. So, it was a time to clean, repair, regroup and relax a bit, particularly as the weather was improving and they were not knee-deep in water. Most of the lads in his platoon were all young, a similar age to Bob; however, a few of them had the experience of two major battles.

After a few months of waiting and a few skirmishes against the German lines, which were now further back, the Yorkshire Regiment was called back along the western front to join other units for another big push to rout the German invaders. This became known as the Battle of Cambrai and was the first massed tank attack, a great shock to the Germans who were terrified at the sight of these great metallic beasts.

Bob said to his men, "What a relief not to be shot at as we leave the trenches. Fix bayonets and keep behind a tank until we reach a German dugout."

It was much easier for the infantry to be advancing quickly and pushing back the Hun. The platoon fought well, killing Germans who fought on or taking many prisoners. The battle was a victory for the allies, the death rate was low and the Germans were again subdued for a time.

The war at sea was also raging, particularly in the Atlantic where the U-boats of the German Navy were creating havoc on the Merchant fleets. Sarah's friend Jim was an engine room officer onboard the Battlecruiser *HMS Calypso*. Due to communication problems at sea, Sarah had not heard from Jim for some time and was worried about his wellbeing. On 17 November, the cruiser was involved in the Battle of Heligoland Bight, out in the North Sea. A direct hit from a German battleship killed all the personnel on the bridge, including the captain, and unfortunately, the shell caused damage near the engine room where Jim was injured. The wounded could be given emergency treatment by the ship's medical staff.

Jim had a chest and head wound so he needed further treatment ashore. The ship managed to limp back to Portsmouth with one of the junior officers in command. The wounded could then be sent ashore to the naval hospital where they could be treated further by the specialist staff. Jim was able to recover, gradually getting better. Sarah was overjoyed when she received a letter from Jim, telling her he was in hospital and apologising for the delay in writing to her.

Chapter 6
1918

Christmas 1917 was a time of peace in the trenches; both sides celebrated the birth of Christ. Bob and his men settled down to open parcels and letters from home.

"Look," said Bob to his corporal John Helmsley, "my girlfriend has sent me some Christmas cake she has made herself and my mum has sent some scones. What a treat! It would be good to be home again, John."

"Yes," he replied. "I live in Thirsk. We would be going out carol singing tonight round all the pubs in the town to raise money for the local hospital so that poor people can be treated. I've got some cake too, my mum's special chocolate cake, we could share."

"Of course," said Bob, "how about getting the lads to sing some carols tonight to remind them of home?"

They sang carols in their damp gruesome trenches and to their surprise, when they sang 'Silent Night Holy Night', they heard the German lads singing with them. On Christmas day, both sides of no man's land wished each other a merry Christmas and a happy new year. Bob thought a lot of lads on both sides would rather give up and go home.

The Germans as a last-ditch attempt launched a spring offensive with hurricane bombardments and infiltration techniques on a sixty-mile front. It nearly worked but for the combined strength of the allied forces which repelled the advance. This was followed by what was termed the Hundred Days Offensive, a combined allied army of tanks, aircraft artillery and infantry pushed the Germans back until they had to surrender. It was relentless. Bob and his regiment were involved in the surrender of the German troops — they just gave up; they had had enough.

On the eleventh hour of the eleventh month, an armistice was signed by the allies and German leaders. It was completed in a railway carriage owned by the supreme allied commander, French General Ferdinand Foch at Le Francport outside Compiegne.

The German forces were stripped of their weapons and marched back over the Rhineland into Germany. It took two years for the peace negotiations to be finalised. In this time. troops were gradually heading back to their homelands. Bob and the remaining soldiers of the Yorkshire Regiment were at last ordered to return to England; however, Bob and some of the lads had come down with a fever. They were made to stay, in quickly made field hospitals to recover from a combination of sore throats, headaches and loss of appetite. It was quickly termed La Grippe. Later, it was to become known as the Spanish flu, a flu pandemic of the H1N1 influenza A virus that infected five hundred million people worldwide and killed up to fifty million. No one knew of its origin. Some said it had come from America with their forces, but this was not ever established as true. Because it was first reported in neutral Spain, it became known as Spanish flu.

After three days, Bob and most of the lads were feeling better. The doctors said they seemed fit enough to return home. There was a number of lads from different regiments ready to return, so after a week of waiting, trucks came to take them to Calais where a troop ship would take them to Portsmouth. The instructions on arrival, were for all services to return to their own barracks. Bob returned by rail to Richmond in Yorkshire. Most of the troops were either demobilised or asked to stay on as permanent soldiers, a choice given to Bob. His commanding officer called him in to see him and asked him personally to consider a career in the army as they considered him a born leader with an outstanding record for his age. He said he would like time to consider it. He was given a fortnight's leave to return home to think it over.

Sarah and the WAACs had made a tremendous contribution to the war effort; in fact, women throughout Britain had replaced men in many roles to allow the release of men to fight. Sarah returned with her regiment to Aldershot where they were demobilised and later would be temporarily disbanded. Her first thoughts were to meet up with Jim before returning home to Stokesley. Jim had been released from hospital and sent home to recuperate. By the time Sarah reached Whitby, he was about back to normal. They had a nice day out in Whitby and Sarah was introduced to Jim's family. Unfortunately, Mr Hutton, Sarah's granddad, had had a stroke so her gran was eager for her to come home to take over the running of the pharmacy.

As they departed, Jim said, "I have to return to Portsmouth to give a report on the battle, but I will soon be released when I will come over to Stokesley to meet your family."

After a kiss and cuddle. Sarah said, "I love you. I am so glad the war was over."

He replied, "I love you too. I am happy we both survived."

Sarah went straight to her grandparents' shop on arrival, they were overjoyed to see her safe return. Granddad's stoke had been a shock; however, he was recovering from it well and would soon be able to help in the shop a little.

Emily and Ted had worked tirelessly with their field ambulance at various positions along the western front. Their main job had been patching up the wounded and caring for the dying.

"What a relief to have no more of those poor wounded lads," said Emily.

Ted agreed, saying, "I could sleep a week, let me know when we can move out."

It was not to be. Just when they thought they could soon return home, many of the young soldiers were coming down with the dreaded fever. The medics were called up to care for the sick instead of the wounded, and it was some months before they could pack up and return home.

On their arrival in Portsmouth, Emily received a telegram from home to say her granddad, Dr Evans, was seriously ill with the Spanish flu, which had turned to pneumonia.

Emily said, "I must go home to Llangollen."

Ted replied, "I will go home to Nantwich to see my parents then come over to see you and meet your family."

They arranged the leave they were due, then travelled to their homes by rail and taxi. Emily was greeted by her grandma, who was happy to see she was well, then hugged her and cried bitterly.

"Your granddad is very ill in hospital, you must go and see him."

He had been treating a number of his patients who had the very virulent flu and caught it himself. The Spanish flu pandemic was to cause the deaths of two hundred and twenty-eight thousand people of all ages in Britain.

Emily was soon at the local hospital where she was well-known and ushered in to see her granddad. He looked very ill; however, he managed to talk when he saw Emily. She briefly told him her story and how she was now engaged to Captain Dr Ted Mills. He smiled and told her he loved her and had loved her father and would like to see her brother and sister. She told him about how courageous they both were and how she had found out how her brother had won the DCM. Emily left the hospital leaving her grandma at the bedside so she could send telegrams to her siblings.

Bob had returned home to see Cathy and his family at the farm, they had a reunion party. June invited her parents and Sarah over from Stokesley. Her father was much improved from his stroke but it had left him a little unsteady; one side of his body was slightly paralysed so he could not drive. Sarah drove the car to the farm. On entering the farm, they were all delighted to see her and she was delighted to see Bob. The conversation flowed at the party.

Bob said, "How Sally and Tommy have grown!"

Bill remarked, "They were a great help on the farm since a number of my farmhands have gone to war and never returned."

Milly was now engaged to Will and showed off her ring.

"How is he?" asked Bob. "I must go and see him."

"He has recovered well although he has a slight limp," said Milly. "He has applied to go into the police force and hopefully take over from his dad."

Grandma Hutton said she wondered how Emily was, the last she had heard she was on her way back from France after treating the lads who had got the flu. June said a number of people in the village had got the flu and two people she knew had died. She was grateful, however, that none of them had got it and she would try and keep it that way. June and Milly had put on a delicious spread so they had a great time, together again after the terror of war. Bill said they had worked hard on the farm to help the war effort and had supplied the troops at the front.

As the night wore on, it was time for Sarah and her grandparents to return home. The party broke up with the usual good wishes and "see you soon" cries from everyone. Bob walked back to the village with Cathy and Milly went with them to see Will. They all went to the pub for a drink where Bob filled Will in on the platoon's movements after Will was wounded and said he was a lucky lad to be engaged to Milly.

Bob said he would see Cathy home then pick up Milly on the way back to the farm. Bob and Cathy strolled over towards the general store, stopping at the big oak tree on the village green. They kissed and hugged each other until Bob got down on one knee and said to Cathy, "I did not want to say this till the war ended, but I have always meant to say you are the one I have always loved. Will you marry me?"

"I thought you would never ask," replied Cathy. "Yes."

Bob said, "We will get a ring tomorrow."

Chapter 7
1920

First thing the next morning, Bob was helping with the milking before breakfast when the telegraph boy arrived with a telegram for him. June took it to him. They all wondered what it could be.

It said, *'Come quickly — Granddad Evans very ill — pneumonia — love Emily.'*

Bob said he must go to see his granddad. They all agreed he should and while Bob was changing to go, June quickly made him some breakfast. He had just sat down when Sarah walked in with a telegram in her hands.

"This has come from Emily."

"We know," said Bob. "I received one, I was just getting ready to go to Llangollen."

"Good," said Sarah, "I will drive us there."

Bob told her about his engagement plans, then asked Milly to go to see Cathy and tell her he would be back as soon as he could, she would understand.

After an uneventful journey, they arrived at their grandparents' house to find a message on the door telling them to come to the hospital. At the hospital, they were taken by a nurse to see their granddad. Outside the ward, they met Emily talking to a man they did not recognise at first, then Bob realised who it was.

"Hello, this is Ted, my fiancé."

They shook hands with Ted and kissed their sister. Granddad Evans was very ill but he recognised his grandchildren. They all kissed him and then introduced Ted, who knew he was in a bad way. They shook hands and Granddad whispered to him, "Look after my girls, won't you?"

"Yes," said Ted, and he seemed to know he would.

At that, he fell asleep. It was time to leave for the night, but they agreed to stay close. Grandma would not leave his side and fell asleep next to him. He never woke up. When Grandma awoke, he had gone. They were all upset at his passing and agreed to stay to help prepare for the funeral. Messages went out to inform the family of the date of the funeral. All the family from England and Wales turned up to see him off. The church was packed with people; many of whom were the hospital staff and patients who he had treated so well.

Emily stayed in Llangollen with her grandma and got a job at the local hospital again. Dr Ted applied to replace Dr Evans and was given the job as the local GP. They were married a month later when all the family gathered together, this time to celebrate a joyous occasion. A honeymoon was arranged for a few days in London, they would go abroad at a later date. They would remain in Llangollen and bring up three children, two boys, David and Simon and a girl Julie.

Bob returned to Hutton Rudby, called in at the shop and arranged to take Cathy to Harrogate for a day out and to get a ring. Next day, they set off in the shop van, out on the old A19 and down to Ripon, where they stopped for a coffee, then on to Harrogate. At Ogdens of Harrogate, Cathy selected a beautiful gold diamond ring. She put it on and kissed Bob with applause from the jewellery staff. A new café had opened on Cambridge Crescent called Betty's, owned by a Swiss chocolatier who had married a Harrogate girl. They had a delicious meal at the café, before walking round the shops and valley gardens. It was a lovely day out. On their return home, they discussed their future plans.

On his return to barracks, Bob had decided what he would do. He asked to see his commanding officer, Major Gordon. He entered his office and said to the major, "I like army life but I need a change after the war. Would it be possible to come back a few times a year and be in reserve?"

"What a good idea," said the major. "I will see the colonel, there are few more chaps like you and we could recruit more and you could help to train them. Good luck to you, Sergeant Evans. I will be in touch."

So, Bob was a civilian again, he spent his time, to earn a living, working on the farm and often helping Cathy and her mum in the shop.

A month or so later, a message came from the regiment to say they were forming reserve units and would he like his name put forward for officer training. He would receive pay for his officer and reserve training. Because of his experience, the officer training would take three months at Catterick camp. He would then take up a position as a platoon commander part-time. Bob agreed to do the training, which he completed with excellent results. He was kitted out with his lieutenant's uniform at Richmond. He would then report for reserve training as required and be on call if needed. After his training, he promised Cathy they would marry. They agreed that Bob would move in with her and her mother, who was having trouble with her arthritis. When not at camp, he would work in the shop. The area above the shop was large with four bedrooms so it would be ideal.

Sarah was working in the pharmacy when Jim turned up, he was now demobbed and had come over from Whitby to see her and meet her family. Jim got on well with the Huttons. After a nice evening meal, the couple went out for a walk. They sat on a bench in the park where Jim said, "I have waited a long time to say this, will you marry me?"

Sarah kissed him and whispered, "Of course."

Then Jim presented her with a lovely diamond ring he had bought from W. Hammonds of Church Street in Whitby. It fitted perfectly; Jim had found out her ring size.

They got married in the parish church in Stokesley a few months after Emily and Ted. All the family attended on both sides. Some of Jim's naval friends turned in up in uniform to give them a guard of honour. It was a joyful occasion. Bob and Cathy and Will and Milly announced their wedding dates that had been arranged so as not to clash with each other.

Sarah was to work in the chemist shop and take over from her granddad fully when he retired. Jim got a job at a big engineering firm called Head Wrightson, they were to build the Thames Barrier at a later date. They had found a two-bedroomed house they liked not far from the shop so Sarah could walk to work. Jim bought a motor bike to get to work; however, as the family came, he eventually was persuaded to use a car. Within a few years, they had a girl who was called Mary after Sarah's mother, followed by a little boy Sam. There was a flat above the shop where Sarah's grandparents lived but even after Granddad died, it was not big enough for a growing family. Both Sarah and Jim had a good income so they were able to buy a detached house in the next street to the shop where they lived for the rest of their lives.

Will and Milly got married just before Bob and Cathy, another lovely day of celebration. Will was now a village policeman and had taken over from his dad. His mum and dad had moved to a bungalow down by the school, so they lived in the police house. Milly would still help her mum and dad at the farm. They had two children; a boy first called John after Will's Granddad and a girl they named Jean.

Bob and Cathy got married in the Baptist chapel where they had attended as children. The church was packed. Bob's family all attended and Cathy had a number of aunties and uncles with their children. Further, some of the men from Bob's platoon were invited. They had a memorable day with a reception in the village hall. For their honeymoon, they spent a week in Llandudno where his mum and dad had met and a place he had gone to as a child. It was a friendly hotel they stayed in, on the sea front overlooking the pier and the promenade.

After what came to be known as the Great War, there was a radical transformation of British society, many old attitudes were swept away. The Liberal Party under Lloyd George collapsed and the Labour Party under Ramsey MacDonald, backed by the unions and hence the working man, became the main challenger to the Conservatives. The Conservatives with Stanley Baldwin as Prime Minister proved to be a steady government, bringing in a mixture of strong social reforms that kept them in power. As leisure, literacy, wealth, ease of travel and a broadened sense of community grew, there was more time and interest in all sorts of activities. The talkies or cinema, dance halls and music halls as well as sporting activities developed and increased.

Llandudno had developed its centre to attract more holiday makers; it now boasted a cinema, a dance hall, an art gallery and an open-air theatre. Bob and Cathy had a great time; they took the tramway up to the summit of the Great Orme and even managed to get to Conwy to see the castle. Cathy loved their time in Llandudno, she always remarked that their first child was conceived in Wales and born in Yorkshire; therefore, was a Welsh Yorkshire man and to some extent he was. They returned home where Bob said to Cathy, "I promise you, we will return to Llandudno with our children one day."

Within the allotted time, sure enough a child was born on 15 June 1924, named George David Evans.

Chapter 8
1930

George or Georgie as he was called as a little boy, soon grew to be a tough little toddler, who took a lot of his parents' time up. He was a constant delight to his dad. Bob had to help in the shop a lot more; although when he was away on military duties, Auntie Milly would help out and sometimes Gran June would look after Georgie up at the farm. Bob would still go up to the farm to help out when needed, although not so often now that Sally and Tommy had left school. They both wanted to work on the farm. Bill was more than happy to have them. He was hoping they would take over more so he and June could relax a bit. Life on the farm was becoming easier. Bill had managed to buy a Ferguson tractor and it proved a great help for lifting and field work.

Bob decided he had better learn to drive so he could drive the tractor when required. Further, he could do with buying a car to get him back and forward from the base at Richmond and take the family out in comfort. Cathy agreed to take him out in the van, she had been taught by her dad. On a Sunday afternoon, when the shop was closed, they would take little Georgie and drive round the Dales, often stopping for a picnic or a country walk. It was while out driving one Sunday that they stopped and parked on a lonely stretch of road near Glaisdale. They set off along a path up over a hill where they looked down on a lake, which they found out later was a bomb crater from the war which had filled with water.

Bob remarked, "This reminds me of the craters left after the battle of Messines."

"Really?" said Cathy. "But it's lovely here."

"Yes," Bob replied, "it does make a difference."

It was later to be called the Blue Lagoon. Georgie loved it, they had a picnic and he was able to paddle and play while his parents kept watch and relaxed in the summer sunshine.

Soon, Bob was an accomplished driver of the van, the tractor and the farm truck.

Bob and Will often met up and had a drink in the pub. One evening, Bob said, "I have been thinking, we should have something to remember the lads and men of the village who gave their lives in the war."

That started with them both going round the village and neighbouring farms to ask for donations to build a war memorial. The lord of the manor at Skutterskelfe Hall, later known as Rudby Hall, gave a worthy donation for he had lost a son at the Somme. They built a war memorial on the village green dedicated to the men of the Yorkshire regiment and others from the village area which was inscribed:

In proud and loving memory of the men of Hutton Rudby who gave their lives for honour and liberty, 1914–1919.

It was a proud but sad moment for the families gathered round to see it.

On 12 January 1930, a little baby girl was born to Bob and Cathy, who they called Joan. Two years later, on 16 October, a boy Brian was born. Cathy and Bob agreed that their family was big enough and they should try not to have any more. Joan grew to be a pretty little girl who looked just like her Auntie Sarah. Cathy said she could always twist her dad round her little finger. Brian was most like his dad; he did well at school in most subjects, unlike his brother Georgie who was more interested in sport than any other subject. They were a happy family who helped each other as they grew up, especially when they were able to help in the shop. Their cousins Mary and Sam would often come round from Stokesley at the weekend so they could play together. Further, they would include John and Jean, Milly and Will's children. They went to school with John and Jean and were always in one another's homes, either playing or doing homework. On occasions, Ted and Emily would come over from Wales, when the children would welcome spending time with David, Simon and Julie.

Bob still had to report for duty at the barracks to work with the part-time soldiers now called the territorial army. He was there a couple of nights a week and in the summer at a number of weeks' camp. It was necessary as tactics and armaments were rapidly changing. After a few years, some of the older officers retired and Bob was promoted to captain. It was then with the extra cash and extra children he decided to buy his first car. After some consideration, he settled on a BSA Light Six, an economical vehicle and good on fuel. What a relief to be able to get to places without having to rely on a bus or train!

The annual holiday became common as conditions improved amongst the working class. Political activists complained that more leisure diverted men away from revolutionary agitation. New estates with small inexpensive houses offered gardening as an outdoor recreation. In general, for most people, there was an improvement in their circumstances. However, although King George V appeared hardworking and was admired by most people in Britain and the Empire, there were certain elements who were not happy with the monarchy. Tourists flocked to the seaside resorts; Blackpool, for example, hosted a million visitors a year by 1930.

Bob, as promised, took his family on holiday to Llandudno in 1934. He packed his new car with all they would need, or so he thought.

Cathy said, "We still have food to go in and there's another case."

Bob said, "Then get in and we'll have to put things on your knees and on the floor."

Somehow, they got everything in the car, then waving bye to Cathy's mum and Milly, who was to help in the shop, they moved off in the direction of Wales.

They had hired a cottage just outside Llandudno, overlooking the bay. On the way, they had promised to make a detour to call in and see Emily and family in Llangollen. After a happy, few hours seeing their Welsh family and having a welcome break, they reached the cottage after a pleasant journey through North Wales.

It was an ideal cottage for a family, the owner lived nearby and was very helpful. A wonderful time was had by all. The children loved the beach and the donkeys, the weather was good with blue skies and very occasional rain — a holiday the children would remember.

The great depression originated on Wall Street in the United States in late 1929 and quickly spread to the rest of the world. The main impact of the slump was felt in 1931. Unlike Germany, Canada and Australia, Britain had not experienced a boom in the 1920s, so the downturn was less severe and ended sooner. However, unemployment was high, especially in the industrial North East.

Bob's family felt the effects of the slump as shop keepers, although not as badly as many in the village. The farms had to keep going to feed the nation as always. People were mainly good and helped each other as before.

Chapter 9
1936

Bob had to pass through Northallerton on his way to Richmond. It was on such an occasion that he stopped to see the Jarrow Crusade march past on their way to stop in the county town of Northallerton. By this time, unemployment was lower in general, but was still bad in the industrial north. Two hundred unemployed men made a highly publicised march from Jarrow to London in a bid to show the plight of the industrial poor. Although much romanticised by the Left, it marked a deep split in the labour party and resulted in no government action.

The death of King George V on 20 January 1936 was a shock to the nation. He and his wife Queen Mary had been greatly loved. At the procession to George's lying-in state in Westminster Hall, part of the Imperial State Crown fell from the top of the coffin and landed in the gutter as the cortege turned into New Palace Yard. The new King Edward VIII saw it fall and wondered whether it was a bad omen for his new reign. As a mark of respect to their father, four surviving sons of George mounted guard at the catafalque on the night before the funeral.

King George V and Queen Mary had five sons; Edward, Albert, Henry, George and John, also a daughter Mary. John died at the age of thirteen. Mary married Viscount Lascelles and became Princess Royal and Countess of Harewood in Yorkshire and had many involvements in Yorkshire life. Henry became Duke of Gloucester. George, the youngest surviving son, became Duke of Kent. Edward became king but was never crowned. He abdicated in favour of love to the American woman Mrs Simpson and was later given the title of Duke of Windsor.

Albert became Duke of York, married Elizabeth Bowes Lyon and had two girls Elizabeth and Margaret. On 11 December 1936, he became king being next in line to his elder brother. He became King George VI at his coronation on 12 May 1937.

Tommy worked on the farm with his father Bill, he was now twenty-nine. He had been very keen on athletics at school and had joined the local athletics club. There he had won races in the 100 and 400 metres events first in local events then in national events. Running had become part of his life and took up most of his free time. Bill and June encouraged him and took him to events until he could go on his own. Bob would go with him to support him when he could. They were overjoyed when he was picked to represent the Great Britain team at the 1928 Olympics in Amsterdam. Although he did not win any individual events, he did well, reaching the finals in the 100 and 400 metres; however, he did win a bronze medal in the 4x100-metre relay.

Athletics in GB were improving. By 1932, at the Los Angeles Olympics, the team was stronger and again Tommy was in the team. This time, he did well and was fourth in the 400-metre race. In the 4x400-metre relay, he won a silver medal.

At home, the family gathered on his return to celebrate his success.

Bill said, "Will you continue to train for the next Olympics?"

"No," said Tommy. "I will leave it for the younger ones coming behind. They have asked me to supervise the team for the 1936 games of the XI Olympiad in Berlin."

On 1 August 1936, the games started. Tommy had arranged for Bill and Bob to be there. It was a wonderful opening ceremony. Bill, in particular, found it amazing. He had never been out of the country before, they all had a marvellous time. One of the highlights was to see Jessie Owens from America win four gold medals in the 100metres, the 400metres, the 100metres relay and the long jump — a remarkable achievement. The other was for Tommy to see his 4x400-relay team win the gold medal and Godfrey Brown a silver medal in the 400-metre individual event.

Unfortunately, Hitler saw the games as an opportunity to promote his Nazi Party ideals of supremacy and anti-Semitism. Germany, however, was top of the ranking with eighty-nine medals, America was second and GB tenth out of thirty-two countries competing. It was to be the last Olympics for twelve years because of the hostilities. London held the 1948 Games of the XIV Olympiad.

The coronation of George VI and Elizabeth his wife took place on 12 May 1937, which had been the planned date of the proposed coronation of Edward VIII.

Many of the regiments of the British Empire were represented in the procession. Bob as a reserve officer and WW1 veteran, holding a DCM, was selected by his regiment to be part of the contingent to represent the Yorkshire Regiment in the procession. They were treated well. A coach took them down to an old house just outside London which had been used as a hospital during the war. A good night was enjoyed by all. Next morning, they were up bright and early, welcomed a clear day and were driven into London. An assembly point was allocated to them ready for the procession.

It was a tremendous celebration, not only a sacred anointing and formal crowning of the king and queen but also a public spectacle which was planned as a display of the British Empire. Heads of states from many countries were present and guests were invited from across the Empire. The procession headed first to Westminster Abbey then returned back to Buckingham Palace. There was a total of 32,000 service people on parade in splendid dress uniforms, both mounted and on foot from every part of the Empire, the streets were lined with 20,000 police officers. Many onlookers marvelled at the sight of the various regiments and their bands, the pipes and drums of the Scots and massed bands of the Guards Regiments making a stirring sound that would be remembered by many for years to come.

There was great jubilation throughout the land, most places had flags and posters to put up. In Bob's village, June and Sally had gone down to Cathy's shop on the green where Sarah and the children had already arrived with the children. They were all very excited. They set about decorating the area and assembling tables and chairs. Most of the villagers had prepared homemade sandwiches and cakes. What a party they had on the green with everyone having a splendid time. There was lemonade and dandelion and burdock for the children and the pubs in the village supplied barrels of beer. Some were a little bit worse for wear the next morning. Bill and Tommy found it hard to get up to do the milking as they were late to get to bed. Good times.

Chapter 10
1939

Winston Churchill was a politician, army officer and writer. He saw action in India, the Sudan and the Boer War. At the beginning of the First World War, he was appointed First Lord of the Admiralty; however. due to the downfall of the Gallipoli campaign, he resigned and spent the rest of the war from 1917 on the western front serving with the Royal Scots Fusiliers. During much of the 1930s, he sought to portray himself as an isolated voice warning of the need to re-arm against Germany.

When Neville Chamberlain replaced Stanley Baldwin as prime minister in May 1937, he did not bring Churchill into the government — that was a mistake. Churchill was a fierce critic of Chamberlain's appeasement of Hitler. He wrote that the government was faced with a choice between 'war and shame' and having chosen shame, would later get war on less favourable terms. Churchill's reputation was probably at its lowest point in 1937–1938, but by 1939, after Germany had absorbed Austria and conquered Czechoslovakia, he was seen as having been proven right. When Germany invaded Poland in September

1939, Chamberlain appointed Churchill to the Cabinet as the First Lord of the Admiralty. It was clear that war was looming and that Germany had the world's most powerful military. Appeasement with Germany was the government's policy, but after the blitzkrieg on Poland, Neville Chamberlain stood firm and Britain and France declared war. The British Commonwealth followed London's lead.

After British forces failed to prevent the German occupation of Norway in April 1940, Chamberlain lost the support of many members of his conservative party. On 10 May, Hitler invaded the Low Countries — Belgium, Luxembourg and the Netherlands — then France. The same day, Chamberlain formally lost the confidence of the House of Commons and handed in his resignation.

Churchill was called upon to replace him. On meeting the king, Churchill wrote:

His Majesty received me most graciously and bade me sit down. He looked at me searchingly and quizzically for some moments and said, "I suppose you don't know why I have sent for you?" Adopting his mood, I replied, "Sir, I simply couldn't imagine why." He laughed and said, "I want to ask you to form a government." I said I would certainly do so.

Winston Churchill was made Prime Minister.

At the outbreak of war in 1939, Bob was told to get all the men in the reserve units ready for full-time combat. Once they were ready, they would join a division in France. The main job for Bob, his officers and NCOs were to see that new recruits who were joining up for the first time were ready for battle.

On 2 September, General Lord Gort was appointed to command the BEF, British Expeditionary Force, to meet up with the French Army with the intention of stopping the German advance. A number of divisions consisting of regiments from across the country were to head to various parts of Northern France. After a fierce resistance, it was obvious the German forces were better equipped, both in manpower but also with superior Panzer tank divisions and over whelming air power. For several months, the Germans were held back until it was necessary to call a retreat. The Battle of France was almost over.

An evacuation took place at Dunkirk, the Germans failed to capture the town on 31 May 1940, because the French and the British rear guard held the Germans back while the last troops were evacuated just before midnight on 2 June. The defending troops began to fall back slowly. By 3 June, the Germans were two miles from Dunkirk and at 10.20 on 4 June, the Germans hoisted the swastika over the docks. Before Operation Dynamo, when a flotilla of little ships went to rescue the troops stranded on the beaches, 27,936 men were embarked from Dunkirk; most of the remaining 198,315 men, a total of 224,320 British troops along with 139,079 French and some Belgian troops were evacuated from Dunkirk between 26 May and 4 June 1940. Much of their equipment, vehicles and heavy weapons had to be abandoned. Two other evacuations took place at a similar time, Operation Cycle from Le-Havre and Operation Ariel from St Nazaire and Nantes. A remarkable feat of rescue for the BEF.

Although it was sad that a number of Bob's recruits from the Yorkshire Regiment had lost their lives in France, some returned to regroup and prepare for the next onslaught. It was expected that Hitler would cross the channel; however, the invasion came by air. On 10 July 1940, the air battle for Britain began when the Royal Air Force defended the UK against large-scale attacks by Nazi Germany's air force the Luftwaffe.

Bob had been unhappy at not being more involved in the action, he told Cathy he had to do more for his country. She replied by telling him he had done enough in the last war but she understood his need to be more active. He was soon to have his wishes fulfilled when a request for volunteers for a special service was called. The request was initially restricted to serving army soldiers; however, by the autumn of 1940, more than 2000 men had volunteered. Bob and one of his sergeants volunteered and were immediately excepted and asked to command a new troop after training. The men were organised into a Special Service Brigade which was quickly expanded into twelve units, which became known as commandos. At first, these men were only on secondment from their units, they retained their own regimental cap badges and remained on the regimental roll for pay. Later, they would be formed into the Royal Marine Commandos.

Winston Churchill had called for a force to be assembled and equipped to inflict casualties on the Germans and bolster British morale. They must be specially trained troops of the hunter class who could develop a reign of terror down on the coasts of German-occupied Europe. The new force must hit sharp and quick — then run to fight another day.

Bob and Sergeant Jack White were requested to get up to Scotland to a place called Achnacarry with strict instructions not to tell anyone, not even their close relatives. This would be the elite commando training grounds. The training regime was innovative and physically demanding and far in advance of normal British Army training. All ranks on arrival were told of the demands of the course and that any man who failed to live up to the requirements would be returned to his unit. The depot staff were all hand-picked, with the ability to outperform any of the volunteers.

Training and assessment started immediately on arrival, with the volunteers having to complete an 8-mile march with all their equipment from Spean Bridge railway station to the commando depot. Exercises were conducted using live ammunition and explosives to make training as realistic as possible. Physical fitness was a pre-requisite, with cross country runs and boxing matches to improve fitness. Speed and endurance marches were conducted up and down the nearby mountain ranges and over assault courses that included a zip-line over Loch Arkaig, all the while carrying arms and full equipment. Training continued day and night with river crossings, mountain climbing, weapons training, unarmed combat, map reading and small boat operations. Living conditions were primitive in the camp. Bob and Jack were housed in a Nissen hut where they were responsible for their own cooking. Correct military protocols were enforced, officers were saluted and uniforms had to be cleaned, with brasses and boots shining on parade. At the end of each course, the final exercise was a simulated night beach landing using live ammunition. Bob and Jack both did well and were recognised as good leaders. Bob was put in charge of a trained unit with Jack as his sergeant. It was called the small-scale raiding force, No 62 Commando, a fifty-five-man unit which came under the operational control of the Special Operations Executive (SOE). They would carry out raids planned by the SOE. As a raiding force, they did not carry the heavy weapons of a normal infantry unit. The weapons used were small arms such as the Fairbairn-Sykes Fighting Knife and the Colt 45 pistol, fire support was provided by the Bren light machine gun, the Thompson submachine gun or the lighter Sten gun.

Before their first raid, the unit was allowed a short rest; however, they could not go off the depot as no one could know of their movements. Bob managed to borrow a car and went to the nearest pub and bought a barrel of beer, cigarettes and food such as scotch pies, sausage rolls and of course haggis. What a party they had for as the saying goes 'eat, drink and be merry for tomorrow you may die,' of course, no one knew what their objective would be or who would survive. One of the units began parachute training and would eventually become the Parachute Regiment.

On the farm, with Tommy and most of the farmhands gone off to enlist, it was difficult for Bill to manage on his own. June and Sally worked hard and sometimes their grandchildren George, Joan and Brian would come over to help. George had just left school and like his father wanted to work at the farm. He was also eager to join up when he was old enough. They needed more help as Bill was now in his sixties and had worked hard all his life.

Women would play an increasing role in many jobs, replacing men called up to the military. In order to grow more food, more help was needed on the farms and so the government started the Women's Land

Army, commonly known as Land Girls. The majority of the Land Girls already lived in the countryside but more than a third came from London and the industrial cities of the north of England.

Life on the home front was a significant part of the war effort for all participants and had a major impact on the outcome of the war. Typically, women were mobilised to an unprecedented degree. The government became involved with new issues such as rationing, manpower allocation, home defence, evacuation in the face of air raids and response to the possible occupation by an enemy power.

The Land Army operated to place women with farms that needed workers, the farmers being their employers. Two Land Girls from South Shields and one from Middlesbrough were allocated to Bill's farm. Sheila and Joyce Barnes were twins from Tyneside and Molly Croft was from Teesside, they were all around 18 years old and had volunteered to get away from other jobs. Fortunately, June had enough space in the farmhouse. On their arrival, she placed Molly in the spare bedroom and the twins together in Tommy's room. They were a nice friendly lot of girls who got on well with each other and turned out to be hard workers. Bill and June were relieved to have them, and they soon became part of the family. Molly could drive so she could use the tractor while they all mucked in with the many jobs needed throughout the seasons. Farming was hard work for girls from the towns.

Sam, the son of Bob's sister Sarah and her husband Jim, had done very well at school and had achieved high marks in his final exams. Sam was good at most sports but had done well at cross country running, gaining many top awards. Growing up with other men in the family who were involved in the services, he had always been determined to go into the army like his Uncle Bob. His parents were not very happy with the idea when hostilities had started; however, they understood that he was determined to be involved. Sam had applied for officer training at the Royal Military Academy Sandhurst and was accepted as a suitable candidate. Sandhurst, Berkshire, was a British Army military academy for training of officers for the British and Indian Armies. At this time, India was still part of the British Empire. Sam had just finished his first year at Leeds University where he was an undergraduate in Metallurgy. Further, he had joined the University Officers' Training Corps. At the outbreak of war, a request had gone out to all Army Training Corps for suitable candidates to apply for officer selection. Like so many at this time, Sam had decided his first duty was to help his country, he had decided to go for army officer training after graduating but felt he was needed now.

Sandhurst develops leadership in cadets by expanding their character, intellect and professional competences to a level demanded of an army officer on his first appointment through military training and education. Sam was to embark on the Regular Commissioning course for direct entry officers which lasts forty-four weeks; however, due to the war it was accelerated. The cadets were asked to work longer hours to complete the course sooner.

After receiving his letter of appointment to report for training, Sam was given the option by the university to return to his studies at a later date. His first visit before heading for Sandhurst was to call in to Stokesley to see his parents and let them know the details of his decision and training schedule.

On arrival at Sandhurst, Sam and the other two hundred cadets were given an introduction to the Academy by the commandant, an officer of major general rank. Each cadet was assigned to a platoon of twenty-five cadets within a company of a hundred cadets. The companies are given names; Sam was in Ypres company. Platoons are commanded by captains, with a colour sergeant who takes the main burden of day-to-day training. The RMAS entrusts the majority of officer training to senior non-commissioned officers (experienced soldiers).

The first day after the introduction, they were kitted out and allowed to settle into their rooms. The evening meal was a time for Sam to get to know some of the other cadets who had come from most parts of the UK.

The next morning at six o'clock, they were in for a shock. They were ordered to dress in fatigues and to report for drill before breakfast. The basic army training, which, by reputation, are the most gruelling, had started and for the next five weeks they were put through hell. This would sort out any unsuitable candidates and toughen up the cadets. Sam and most of his platoon did well and were noticed to be the best in the company.

The following months consisted of leadership and conflict studies, decision making and battle techniques etc. During this time, they were sent on route marches, fully equipped and undertook mock battles. Sam had got to know his platoon members well, in particular John Ellis who was from Banger and had studied civil engineering at Cardiff University. By the end of the training, they were determined to stay together and would try to be selected for the same regiment.

Sarah and Jim with Bob managed to get down for the passing out parade when the cadets were commissioned as officers. Sam was awarded the sword of honour as he was considered the best overall cadet on his course. John, Sam's close friend was awarded the King's Medal as the cadet who achieved the highest scores in military practical and academic studies on his course. After the parade, both Sam and John's parents met and arranged to take the boys out for a meal in a local pub. They had a great time talking about past times and the present conflict.

Bob raised a toast, saying, "I wish you both good luck and may God keep you safe when you are facing the enemy."

They were given leave to go home where they would soon receive their orders to join a regiment. Sam travelled back with his parents', and Bob had to go on from Sandhurst to join his unit.

Sam had a few days at home seeing his friends and relatives before receiving his orders. He was asked to join a new Battalion of the Sherwood Foresters (Nottinghamshire and Derbyshire Regiment) many new Battalions were being formed due to the hostilities. Officers were needed to help train the new recruits and lead them going forward.

Sam and John, his close friend at Sandhurst, had expressed their wish to be in the same regiment. Their wish had been granted by the commandant who had made sure they were together. John phoned Sam to tell him the good news that they would meet up at Normanton Barracks in Derby.

Sarah's daughter Mary was in her last year at the local Grammar school. A keen swimmer and netball player, she had done well at her school work and wanted to go on to university. The war starting made her think otherwise; she was considering joining the navy like her dad. Mary would later become an officer in the Women's Royal Navy Service, nicknamed the WRENs.

Sam and John met up in the barracks where they were kitted out in their new uniforms as platoon leaders, First Lieutenant the Sherwood Foresters. The following months they, with their experienced training sergeants from other units, had to see to training the raw recruits. Men in the new battalion were from all walks of life and needed to be battle-ready. Some found the training difficult at first, but as time passed, they became an efficient fighting force. Sam who was young compared to some of the men, soon overcame any reluctance to follow his lead by doing everything they had to do, but in most cases better. The final training in battle tactics involved live ammunition. The idea was for two companies to try to capture each other; however, no one was supposed to be injured. The live ammunition were grenades. These were to be released in safe areas overhead of the troops; however, unfortunately accidents did happen. One of the grenades landed near the officers observing the action and Captain Green, who was Sam's company captain, was badly injured with shrapnel. As a result of this, Sam was selected as the candidate for promotion and took over as company captain.

Chapter 11
1940

At this time, the Battle of Britain was taking place in the air above the farm. Dog fights could be seen between *Spitfires* and *Messerschmitts* and often a German bomber would be shot down or sometimes one of our fighters. The action was the same over London and many of the industrial towns and cities. Teesside was a big industrial area, with a large dock for transporting goods from the area. The iron and steel company by Dorman Long, ICI chemical company and all such companies on the North East rivers such as shipbuilding, were a target for the Luftwaffe.

Seeing the raids taking place was a worry for the three Land Girls, who had family in the bombing areas. The twins managed to contact their family who were all safe and well; however, Molly could not contact anyone and was very concerned for her mother, ten-year-old brother and five-year-old little sister. her father was in the forces. George and Molly had become very friendly as they worked together on the farm so George offered to take Molly home to see if her family were all right in Middlesbrough. They borrowed the farm truck and set off to the town which was only a few miles away over the moors and down into Teesside. Molly's home was in the town centre, a house in Wood Street.

As they neared the centre, they could see there had been a lot of damage near the docks. When they turned into the street, a number of houses had been bombed. One of them was number eight, Molly's home — it was gone. On the street side was an air raid shelter.

Molly said, "I hope they got out to the shelter in time. I wonder where they are now."

George said, "Someone may know, what about the neighbours?"

Just then, Mrs Dodd's who was a friend of her mum and lived further up the street came up to them. She told them that they were safe, that after the bombing they had gone to Molly's gran's in Pickering. They had stayed in the shelter all night, then the police had taken them to her gran's. What a relief for Molly, a terrible fear had been removed from her mind. George and Molly went on to Pickering to see the family was safe, they had a short break and some tea with them all, then returned to the farm.

Emily's son David had taken to study medicine like his father and grandfather. David was a gifted boy, had done well at school and was getting on well as a second-year undergraduate at Cambridge University. David had always been interested in flying as a boy, so when he found there was a University Air Squadron, he immediately joined. The main role of the UAS was to attract ambitious and intelligent students into careers such as RAF officers. Primarily, its goal is achieved through offering basic flying training, force development and adventure training to undergraduate students. Most students hold the rank of Officer Cadet. Medicine and dentistry students, on obtaining a cadetship, are commissioned into the RAF in the rank of pilot officer and are offered a salary. Following graduation, cadets are promoted to flying officer while their medical training continues, prior to commencing Initial Officer Training.

On the run up to World War II, the university squadrons were an important source of pilots for the RAF during the Battle of Britain. Because David had done some elementary flying training, he was called up for active service in the middle of studying for his degree. David was sent to Cranwell where he would continue training as a pilot. The time taken to qualify as a pilot could vary. On average, it took between eighteen months to two years. However, due to the urgent need for pilots at the start of the war, it could be as little as six months (150 flying hours). Students progressed through several stages of training. Tests and examinations had to be successfully passed before the next level of instruction could be taken. Initial training provided an induction for cadets to RAF service. Ground instruction also formed the basis for flying training. Topics included mathematics, navigation and the principles of flying. Pupils learnt the basics of how to fly an aircraft such as the *de Havilland Tiger Moth* then, followed by more powerful aircraft such as the *North American Harvard*. After advanced training, final examinations were completed when the pupil received his flying brevet or pilot's wings.

David completed his training in four months. He was a natural pilot. Of course, obtaining pilot's wings did not mark the end of training. Qualified pilots were sent to Operational Training Units to fly *Spitfires* and *Hurricanes* to make them ready for front- line duties.

David was sent to RAF Kenley to join 485 Squadron, where after a few flights in *Spitfires*, he was deemed ready for combat. He did not have to wait long before his first maiden combat flight. David thought the *Spitfire* a dream machine and took to the sky with confidence. The squadron was sent up repeatedly against overwhelming odds. David managed to survive a number of sorties by shooting down ten German fighter and six bomber aircrafts. He was awarded the DFC, Distinguished Flying Cross. After six months, the squadron was decimated. Half the original pilots had been killed in action, including the squadron leader. David took over as SL with new pilots to lead.

The primary objective of the German forces was to compel Britain to agree to a negotiated peace settlement. The Luftwaffe was directed to achieve air superiority over the RAF, with the aim of incapacitating RAF Fighter Command. Attacks were made on RAF airfields and infrastructure, they also targeted factories involved with aircraft production. Hitler ordered the preparation of Operation Sea Lion as a potential amphibious and airborne assault on Britain to follow, once the Luftwaffe had air superiority. RAF Bomber Command's night raids disrupted the German preparation of converted barges and the Luftwaffe's failure to overwhelm the RAF forced Hitler to postpone and eventually cancel Operation Sea Lion.

Between 10 July and 31 October, the Battle of Britain raged. Except for a few rests, David was in the air with his squadron, once having to bail out; he had a near-miss when a German bullet hit his engine, but he managed to free his cockpit and jump out. Back at the airfield, he was missed. None of the returning pilots had seen what had happened during the dog fight. Three flyers were missing presumed dead, there was a great cheer from the men when he turned up hours later driven by a pretty girl.

David had landed in a ploughed field. Luckily, the farmer's family had been watching the battle in the sky. The farmer drove over in his tractor and said to him, "We were watching at the time and saw you shoot down two German planes before you had to bail out."

The farmer took him to the farm house where he met his wife and two daughters. David was treated to tea and some farmhouse food which they all enjoyed together. One of the daughters was about David's age. She was called Dorothy or Dot and volunteered to take him back to his base. They got on well together on the way back. David said to Dot he was very grateful and could he call and take her out to dinner. That was the beginning of a life-long friendship.

A few days later, as the squadron worn and weary waited for the alarm to action. All was silent, the battle had been won. Germany proved unable to sustain daylight raids, but their continued night bombing operations on Britain became known as the Blitz. During the Battle of Britain, 544 pilots were killed from Fighter Command compared to 2500 Luftwaffe airmen killed in action.

Impressed by the success of German airborne operations, Winston Churchill directed the War Office to investigate the possibility of creating a corps of 5,000 parachute troops. On 22 June 1940, No 2 Commando was turned over to parachute duties, re-designated the 11th Special Air Service Battalion, with a parachute and glider wing. On 10 February 1941, it became the 1st Parachute Battalion of the Parachute Regiment.

Tommy had stayed at home to help at the farm. Eventually, all able-bodied men were called up for service. Although he could have claimed his was a reserved occupation, but he was determined to go. His mum June was not happy with his decision; however, she said he must do what he thought was his duty. He enlisted at the local recruitment office, where after reviewing his background, the officer-in-charge said he would be ideal to join a new regiment, would he be happy being trained for the Parachute Regiment? Tommy was happy to agree and was soon sent off for training.

Parachute training was a twelve-day course carried out at No. 1 Parachute Training School at RAF Ringway. Recruits initially jumped from a converted barrage balloon and finished with five parachute jumps from an aircraft. Anyone failing to complete a parachute jump was returned to his old unit or transferred to another regiment. Parachute training was not without its dangers; three men were killed in the first 2000 jumps at Ringway. Tommy had no problems and at the end of the course was presented with his maroon beret and parachute wings then posted to a parachute battalion. Airborne soldiers were expected to fight against superior numbers of the enemy who were often equipped with artillery and tanks. So training was designed to encourage a spirit of self-discipline, self-reliance and aggressiveness. Emphasis was given to physical fitness, marksmanship and fieldcraft. A large part of the training consisted of assault courses and route marching. Military exercises included capturing and holding airborne bridgeheads, roads or rail bridges and coastal fortifications. At the end of most exercises, the battalion would march back to their barracks. An ability to cover long distances at speed was expected, airborne platoons were required to cover a distance of fifty miles in twenty-four hours and battalions thirty-two miles.

Tommy was sent to join the 1st Parachute Brigade part of the British 1st Airborne Division which was to take part in Operation Fustian; an operation undertaken during the Allied invasion of Sicily in July 1943. Their objective was the Primosole Bridge across the Simeto River. The intention was for the brigade, with glider-borne forces in support, to land on both sides of the river. They would then capture the bridge and secure the surrounding area until relieved by the advance of the British XIII Corps, which had landed on the south-eastern coast three days previously. The bridge was the only crossing on the river, its capture was expected to speed the advance and lead to the defeat of the Axis forces in Sicily.

Many of the aircraft carrying the paratroopers from North Africa were shot down or damaged due to enemy action and only the equivalent of two companies of troops were landed in the correct location. Tommy with his platoon was part of the correct landing, they assembled and headed for the bridge. Despite being out-numbered by the defending German and Italian forces, they managed to capture the bridge, repulsed attacks and held out till nightfall. The relief force which was short of transport were still a mile away when they halted for the night. By this time, due to casualties mounting and supplies running short, Tommy and his platoon were ordered to relinquish control of the bridge. The following day, the British units joined forces and a Battalion of the Durham Light Infantry, led by the paratroopers, established a bridgehead on the north bank of the river. Tommy was glad the action was over as some of the men he had got to know well had been killed or injured.

He had fought well and on the return to barracks was made a sergeant to lead his platoon who had lost men in the battle.

Operation Slapstick was the code name for a British landing from the sea at the Italian port of Taranto. The operation was planned at short notice so the Airborne division located in North Africa was selected to undertake the mission. However, there was a shortage of aircrafts which meant the division had to be transported across the Mediterranean by ships of the Royal Navy.

Tommy and his corporal John Lawson had become good friends. John said, "I do not like the idea of a beach landing."

Tommy remarked, "It cannot be worse than falling down from the sky and being shot at by a Gerry."

Fortunately, there was little opposition. The shelling from the warships gave enough cover for a successful landing. The Airborne Division soon captured the ports of Taranto and Brindisi on the Adriatic coast, the heel of Italy for the Allies.

The only German forces in the area were elements of the 1st Parachute Division (Fallschirmjäger Division) which engaged the advancing British in ambushes and at roadblocks during a fighting withdrawal north. Tommy and his platoon were advancing north along a major road when they were attacked in a German ambush. Fierce fighting continued, until it was obvious they had to get behind the Germans, and knock out their machine guns. Tommy and John with a few other men managed to manoeuvre round the German lines and attack from the rear, killing the machine gunners and allowing the rest of the platoon to advance. It was a bloody mess. John was badly wounded in the thigh, Tommy had only a superficial wound in the arm, some of the men were killed, but at least the Germans were retreating. The advance continued until by the end of September. The whole Airborne Division had advanced a hundred and twenty-five miles to Froggia. Reinforcements from the two infantry divisions had by then landed behind them, which allowed the airborne troops to be withdrawn to Taranto and later Brindisi. Tommy and John were treated for their wounds and soon after, the division sailed for England in preparation for Operation Overlord.

Tommy was awarded the Military Medal (MM) for his bravery in the action and the Italy Star was awarded to all the men in the platoon.

Before the attack on Pearl Harbour, the Japanese had already begun imperial expansion in China and other territories and islands. The Empire of Japan entered World War II on 27 September 1940 by signing the Tripartite Pact with Germany and Italy. It wasn't until the attack on Pearl Harbour on 7 December 1941 that the United States entered the conflict. They were then so outraged by the attack that they were persuaded to join the global conflict and became involved with the war on all fronts. Over the course of seven hours, the Japanese carried out coordinated attacks on the US-held Philippines, Guam and Wake Island and on the British Empire in Borneo, Malaya, Singapore and Hong Kong. The strategic goals of the offensive, were to cripple the US Pacific fleet, capture oil fields in the Dutch East Indies and so expand the outer reaches of the Japanese Empire.

Hong Kong, Borneo, Malaya and Singapore all surrendered to the Japanese. The Allied armies consisting of British, Indian, Australian and Malay forces were overwhelmed by the sudden attacks due to the superiority of the Japanese forces and encirclement tactics. The Allies lacked air cover and tanks; the

Japanese had air supremacy. The sinking of *HMS Prince of Wales* and *HMS Repulse* led to the east coast of Malaya being exposed to Japanese landings and the elimination of British naval power in the area. This led to the largest surrender of British-led military personnel in history. An estimated 80,000 troops were taken as prisoners of war in Singapore, they were joined with 50,000 troops taken in Malaya. Many were later used as forced labour constructing the Burma railway, the site of the infamous bridge on the River Kwai. The hardships the troops went through in the Japanese prisoner of war camps and in labouring on railway construction was horrific beyond words, few ever returned.

In the Philippines, the Japanese pushed the combined Filipino — American force towards the Bataan Peninsula and later to the island of Corregidor. By January 1942, General Douglas MacArthur and President Manuel L. Quezon were forced to flee in face of the Japanese advance. This was the worst defeat suffered by the Americans, leaving 70,000 prisoners of war.

Chapter 12
1942

Bob and eleven men were part of Operation Barricade. This was Bob's first raid on occupied territory. To perform the sea borne raid, they required a small troop of men and rapid transport. Bob had selected his men and they boarded *HM MTB 344*, a motor torpedo boat nicknamed *'The Little Pisser'* due to its outstanding turn of speed. The objective was an anti-aircraft gun and radar site north-west of Pointe de Saire, south of Barfleur.

They landed on the night of 14 August without being detected. They approached up a steep cliff and being so silent were able to plant explosives around the gun and radar station. A German patrol was heading towards their escape route so they opened fire, killing three and wounding six, before withdrawing without loss to the commandos. As they made their way down the cliff back to the boat, more Germans were alerted, but to no avail; a tremendous explosion was heard. They made it back to the boat and sped off at rapid acceleration, leaving the Germans bewildered. It happened so quickly, the operation was a complete success.

Because of their success, Bob and his hand-picked men were allowed a short break before being selected for another task, Operation Dryad. Bob and Sergeant White had to get their men ready for another night raid using *The Little Pisser* again. Their objective was a raid on the Casquets lighthouse in the Channel Islands. Sailing from Portland, they left at nine p.m., arriving at ten forty-five p.m. because of the outstanding speed of the *MTB 344*. After anchoring, the party rowed ashore, arriving at just after midnight. Bob was the first to leap ashore and tied their boat forward. Jack was in control of the stern-line, which had been attached to the kedge-anchor that had been dropped on approach to prevent the boat being smashed against the rocks. All the landing party made it safely ashore without any damage to the boat.

They made their way through barbed wire up the steep rocky surface to the lighthouse courtyard unchallenged. Once in the courtyard, the group dispersed to their prearranged objectives. Bob and Jack dashed up the spiral staircase to the tower light only to find it unoccupied. The garrison was totally surprised. Three were sleeping, two were just turning in and two others were on duty. The seven Germans were taken prisoner without a shot being fired. One German, who was in charge of the lighthouse operation fainted at the sight of the commandos. Another was initially thought to be a woman because he was wearing a hairnet.

All weapons found were dumped in the sea. The radio was smashed with an axe, they rounded up the prisoners and returned to the boat. The boat was designed to take a maximum of ten people, now with eighteen, it was difficult but they managed to get back to the *MTB*.

Setting sail at 1.35 a.m. with the seven prisoners, some still in their pyjamas, they arrived back at Portland at 3.00 a.m. On their arrival, the prisoners were held for questioning. Several codebooks, logs, diaries and letters which had been found were handed over for analysis. The commandos had captured the lighthouse and its occupants, then departed, leaving no trace that anyone had ever been there.

This was typical of many raids by the commandos on occupied territory and was most annoying to Hitler and his henchmen. Many raids were carried out by the commandos to harass the Germans and prevent their progression; however, the results were not always successful as was the case with Operation Aquatint. Bob and his men were not on that raid, when a landing was made at Sainte-Honorine on the coast of Normandy. Because they were heavily outnumbered, all men involved were lost, except one who managed to escape and reach Spain but was betrayed by a French double-agent and handed to the Germans. After spending nine months in solitary confinement, he was shot.

Early in 1943, No 62 Commando was disbanded and its members dispersed among other formations, some served in the Special Boat Squadron or the Special Air Service. Bob and Jack were to join the newly formed Royal Marine Commando service, with No 47 Commando based in Dorchester. They were part of the 4th Special Service Brigade alongside No 41, No 46 and No 48 Commandos. Bob was to lead a thirty-man section with Jack as his sergeant.

They reported to the marine barracks to be told they were given leave before their next action.

Captain Bob Evans RM returned home after being away for many months. He drove home in his car and arrived in the early evening. What a surprise for Cathy and the children. They were just closing the shop and were delighted to see him. Cathy and the children hugged and kissed him, then they all went into the kitchen where Cathy's mum was making a meal. She gave him a hug and kiss, then they all settled down to a good meal with plenty of chatter about what they all had been doing.

Bob said, "The children have grown since my last visit."

"Yes," said Cathy. "They all wish they could help to fight the Nazis, particularly George."

"Well," Bob replied, "it's hell out there, George, you don't need to get involved. You are already doing essential work on the farm. Take my advice and keep farming."

Cathy said, "Joan and Brian are both doing well at school," and got their reports out to show Bob.

He said, "You have done well. I will let you have some money and take you into Harrogate on Saturday before I go back to barracks."

What a great night they had, singing songs round the piano. They all could sing well; however, Joan had a lovely soprano voice and sang, 'We'll Gather Lilacs in the Spring Again' beautifully.

The next morning, Bob went up to the farm with George, the other children were still at school and Cathy had to run the village shop.

On the way, George said "Dad, I am thinking of getting engaged to Molly, one of the Land Girls I have fallen in love with."

"If you are sure, but before you do, let me meet her."

"My mum and Gran think she is a good girl for me," said George, "and she has become part of the family at the farm."

At the farm, Bob was greeted with the usual kiss and hug from June, who had been his mother as a child and a warm hug from Bill who had treated him as his son. They told him about Tommy, how he had been promoted to sergeant and were hoping to see him home for a visit soon.

"You should pop and see Milly and Will while you are here," said June.

"I was going to meet up with them tonight," replied Bob.

"Come with me," said George, "and meet the Land Girls."

"I'll come with you," said Bill. "Those girls have been a god-send. I need to get the tractor over to the top field for mowing."

Bob met the twins who were in the milking shed. They were delightful with their Geordie accent and keen sense of humour. Molly was mucking out the old horses when George introduced his dad. Bob talked about his time on the farm as they helped to get the horses ready for some ploughing. Once done, Bob said he was off back to the shop, wished them well and whispered to George, "She's a lovely girl."

He was about to leave the farm when who should arrive but Tommy, Staff Sergeant in the Parachute Regiment.

"Nice to see you," said Bob. "I was just off home, you look well. How are you?"

"OK and you?" replied Tommy.

"Grand. I will let you see the others. Will you come down to the pub tonight and we will all meet up?"

"See you down there later, eight o'clock. Be OK."

That night, Bob, Cathy, Will, Milly, Tommy, George and Molly all met up and had a good time talking about family, the war and the future.

Tommy said, "I have only two days' leave before I have to report back."

Bob said, "I have to get back on Sunday too, there is something big going on."

That night, they wished each other a safe future and some struggled home a bit worse for wear.

Next day, Bob took Cathy and the two younger children to Harrogate, they had a good time looking round the shops. Brian bought a penknife and Joan bought a nice fountain pen. They both got sweets although the choice was not great because of the rationing. After Cathy got a new dress and they all said it was lovely, they had lunch in that famous café called Betty's. On the way back to the car, they happened to pass a local shop window that was displaying part of a bomb. It was said to be the only bomb dropped in Harrogate. It fell on the Hotel Majestic with little damage and no one was injured. There were many speculations as to why the bomb had been dropped; one was the bomber crew had been waiters at the Majestic before the war and were getting their revenge. Their journey back took them past an airfield at RAF Dalton which had been bombed and was under repair, which could explain why a bomb ended up in Harrogate.

On Sunday after church and lunch, the family said farewell to their brave soldiers. Cathy was in tears and told Bob to come back safe. Bob and Tommy had to return to their regiments to fight yet again.

When the Germans changed their strategy away from bombing airfields and industrial sights on to the night-time bombing of cities known as the Blitz, David was transferred to No 219 Squadron RAF, also flying from RAF Kenley. He was one of the first to fly the new Bristol Type 156 Beaufighter, a multi-role aircraft. Its large size allowed it to carry heavy armament and early airborne interception radar without major performance penalties. It was a combination of a fighter and a bomber with heavy guns and the capability to fire rockets.

It was radar that proved to be the critical weapon in the night battles over Britain. David with his crew of Pilot Officer Geoffrey Mason (observer) and Flight Sergeant Robert Leyland (air intercept radar operator) became one of the first crews to intercept and destroy an enemy aircraft using on-board radar to guide them to a visual interception when they brought down a Dornier 17 off the Kent coast. Although David and his crew were doing well, the Luftwaffe was still getting through to their targets, taking no more than two- percent losses per mission.

In honour of Hitler's 52nd birthday, 712 bombers hit Plymouth with a record 1,000 tons of bombs. However, as more Beaufighters came into service the following month, twenty-two German bombers were lost with thirteen confirmed to be shot down by Beaufighters.

On one night, London suffered severe damage, but ten German bombers were downed, three by David and his crew. Although they had shot down three bombers, they went for a fourth but were hit by a German fighter. With a wing burning badly, they managed to escape back to Kenley. David warned the airfield they were making an emergency landing with an injured observer. They made it down just in time before the fire spread to the fuel tanks. Once the three flying crew were clear, the ground crew were able to put out the fire and save most of the aircraft.

Within a few months, the Germans had to admit defeat in the skies and the fact that the British people were not demoralised but enraged by the bombing led Hitler to change his plans. He now had his sights set on attacking the USSR with Operation Barbarossa and the Blitz came to an end. Between 20 June 1940 when the first German air operations began over Britain and 31 March 1941, it is recorded the Germans lost 2,265 aircrafts over the British Isles, a quarter of them fighters. At least 3,363 Luftwaffe aircrew were killed, 2,641 missing and 2,117 wounded. A significant number of aircrafts not shot down after they resorted to night bombing were wrecked during landings or crashed due to bad weather.

David had taken Dorothy Barker to dinner on several occasions and they had become lovers and very much in love. David had not thought it wise to get too involved but now the Blitz was over, he would propose. He had leave coming, arranged with Dot's parents to take her up to Llangollen and then met Dot for dinner.

He said to Dot, "I love you and want you, will you be my wife?"

Dot said, "Of course not, don't be silly."

David was taken back at this, but a second later, she said, "Yes, my darling, I love you too."

David then kissed her and said, "I am taking you up to Wales at the weekend to see my parents and Simon and Julie, my siblings. We will buy you a ring at the jeweller's in my home town."

Dot was delighted to be going; due to the war, she had not been away for years.

Early Saturday morning, they set out for Wales. David had bought a Jensen S-type car and liked to drive fast. As a pilot, he was a good driver, not reckless like some of his friends. The weather had turned out fine. They stopped once on the way in a little village and had coffee and scones at a local café. By tea-time, they arrived at Llangollen and parked in the town centre. David took Dot to the jeweller's he knew and there, Dot picked her ring which was a beautiful single diamond set in platinum. She was overcome with joy as they headed to David's home. They arrived to the delight of Emily and the family.

Over the evening meal, they celebrated the engagement and all got to know each other. Dot had trained as a teacher and worked in a primary school, Simon had just finished school and said he was going to Dartmouth college to train for the Royal Navy. Julie was in her last year of school and wanted to be a nurse like her mum. When Julie had taken Dot upstairs to see her bedroom, Emily and Ted told David they thought Dot was a lovely girl and wished him well.

Emily remarked, "But wait for the war to end before getting married."

David said, "That is the plan, we have already decided."

The next day after lunch, they had to return to their jobs in Kenley. After sad farewells and many hugs, and Emily reminding David to "write" and to "come back safe as soon as you can", they set off back.

The 13th Battalion of the Sherwood Foresters was a hostilities-only unit raised in 1940. In 1942, it was sent to India where it was converted to the armoured role as 163rd Regiment Royal Armoured Corps. In common with other infantry battalions transferred to the RAC, the personnel of 163 RAC continued to wear their Foresters cap badge on the black beret of the RAC. This was Sam and John's battalion, they had wanted to be involved in fighting the Germans; however, they were informed of the threat to India from the Japanese and the need to train the new Indian recruits.

The passage to India by troop ship, escorted by British Navy destroyers went without any difficulty, such as submarine or air attack. On arrival in India, the converted Regiment 163 RAC was stationed in Rawalpindi under the command of the 267th Indian Armoured Brigade.

At the outbreak of the Second World War, the Indian Army numbered 205,000 men. Later on, during the war, the Indian Army would become the largest all-volunteer force in history, rising to over two and a half million men in size. The Army of India consisted of the British Indian Army, led by expatriate British officers and the British Army in India, which consisted of British Army units posted to India for a tour of duty.

Sam and John were at first seconded with some of their NCOs to help train the new Indian recruits. The Indian Army was committed to fighting the Japanese Army, they had retreated from Burma to the Indian border. Later after resting and refitting, they made a victorious advance back into Burma as part of the largest British Empire army ever formed. These campaigns cost the lives of over 87,000 Indian servicemen, while another 34,354 were wounded and 67,340 became prisoners of war. Their valour was recognised with the award of some 4,000 decorations and eighteen members of the British Indian army were awarded the Victoria Cross or the George Cross. Field Marshal Claude Auchinleck, Commander-in-Chief of the British Indian Army from 1942, asserted that the British "couldn't have come through both wars if they hadn't had the British Indian Army."

During this time, officers met up with other military and civilian expatriates, meeting in the local clubs and bars. This allowed them to get to know the culture and the correct procedures in society. However, after some months' training, Sam and John were given leave after a hard schedule and the now intense heat of the Indian summer. They travelled by train up to the hill station of Simla, this is where the British would retreat to in the hot weather. Sam and John were able to stay in one of the hotels where they were invited to parties and other activities. The invites often came from the wives and daughters of the older officers.

One evening, a ball had been arranged in the honour of all the new officers. It was at this ball that Sam asked a very pretty young lady to dance. It was love at first sight. She was the daughter of a Major Robert McDonald of the Indian Army, who was married to an Indian lady of high caste. Her name was Ella. They danced until late, then Sam took Ella to her room, with the promise of seeing her to play tennis the next day. The following days, they were always in each other's company apart from when they met up with John and his girlfriend Barbara, a close friend of Ella. One afternoon, Sam had arranged to take Ella on a walk to a beauty spot. With a picnic in his rucksack, they set off along a well-known trail where they reached a magnificent waterfall and large pool with a stream leading downhill. They settled down under a large palm tree to have their picnic.

It was then that Sam said, "Over the last few days, I have fallen in love with you."

Ella replied, "I feel the same way, Sam."

At this, they kissed which led them to making love with total abandonment.

Sam asked, "Will you marry me?"

The answer was, "Yes, with all my love."

On their return to the hotel, Sam braved a meeting with Major McDonald. "I would like your permission to marry your daughter," Sam said. "We are in love and she has agreed to marry me."

The major replied, "Captain Whitehead, I understand your request, and I believe you would be a very good match for my daughter. It is, however, not the time to consider marriage. Wait until the war is over, when if you both feel the same, we will discuss it further."

Sam and Ella both agreed it was good advice, they would see each other whenever they could.

The next day, Sam and John were asked to report back to their regiment, they were needed for special operations. Ella said they would return to Delhi soon where her father had a new posting. They both promised to write. Sam said he would be back for her as soon as he could.

The 163 RAC was reconverted back into the 13th Battalion Sherwood Foresters as a line infantry regiment. Some officers and men were asked to join a Long-Range Penetration Group called the Chindits which would operate behind the Japanese lines in Burma. Sam and John would lead a company as part of the group.

British Army Brigadier Orde Charles Wingate formed the Chindits (named after a Burmese mythical beast, statues of which guarded Buddhist temples) for raiding operations against the Imperial Japanese Army, especially long-range penetration. They would attack Japanese troops, facilities and lines of communication deep behind Japanese lines. Wingate arrived in Burma in 1942 and for two months, as Japanese forces advanced rapidly, toured the country developing his theories of long-range penetration.

A force of 3000 troops, half of which were British, were selected from a number of regiments including the Sherwood Foresters, the King's Liverpool Regiment, the 2nd Gurkha Rifles, the 2nd Burma Rifles and men from the bush warfare school in Burma who formed into 142 Commando. Wingate took charge of the training in the jungles of central India during the rainy season.

This force as long-range penetration units were to be supplied by stores parachuted or dropped from transport aircraft and were to use close air support as a substitute for heavy artillery. Small detachments from the RAF equipped with radios to call in support were attached to each of the columns consisting of three hundred and six to three hundred and sixty-nine men. Each column had nine Bren light machine guns, three two-inch mortars, four anti-tank rifles, two Vickers machine guns and two light anti-aircraft guns. The heavy weapons, radios, reserve ammunition and stores were carried on mules. Each man carried more than seventy-two pounds (thirty-three kg) of equipment which included a Sten gun or rifle, ammunition, grenades, a machete, seven days' rations, a groundsheet, a change of uniform and other assorted necessary items.

Their operations featured prolonged marches through extremely difficult terrain, often undertaken by underfed troops sometimes weakened by diseases such as malaria and dysentery. They would penetrate the jungle on foot, essentially relying on surprise through mobility, to target enemy lines of communication. The main aim was to cause confusion and delay the progression of the Japanese forces into India and ultimately defeat their army in Burma.

Sam and John had their first taste of battle when the Chindits crossed the Chindwin River and faced the first Japanese troops. The Japanese would die rather than be defeated, they were easily outnumbered by the full Chindit force, and many died on both sides. After months of bitter fighting, Sam was ordered to take a column of his men including a detachment of Gurkha's and attack and destroy a communication site deep in the jungle.

They stayed clear of the normal paths through the jungle to enable them to take the Japanese by surprise. The Japanese were building a railway which would enable them to transport their troops and equipment easily. Sam and his men had to cut their way through the jungle with machetes or the Gurkha kukri knife for several days. It was hard going especially when it rained in great downpours. They would camp at night, have meagre rations and get some sleep. At last, they reached the Japanese site in daylight and stealthily surveyed the area. The men sent out returned with a report that as they were looking, a column of Japanese troops had arrived; therefore, the place was well-guarded and they were outnumbered.

"Right," said Sam. "John, we will split into two groups; you take one group and attack from the right of the site, I will take the other group and attack from the left. We will wait until late in the night when most of them are asleep, which should give us the advantage of surprise. I will lead a few men in to lay explosives on the transmitter, stores and barracks. When they go off, we attack."

Night time came with the darkness only found in the jungle. They managed to get some rest, keeping very quiet. Fortunately, they were seasoned troops used to hiding and moving in silence. At midnight, Sam with four Gurkhas, who were expert at sneak attacks, crept in to lay the explosives, then successfully returned to the men to let them off. There was total confusion among the Japanese at first as the British column attacked. All hell broke loose as the Japanese recovered and reached their heavy machine gun posts. Sam led a suicidal attack on the two machine guns and although wounded, fought on till they were blown up with grenades. This action saved many lives; however, the bloody battle continued until a few of the Japanese retreated into the jungle. Many men had died or been wounded. John was one of the dead, a great sorrow to Sam who was wounded in his arm and side. They quickly buried their dead comrades and patched up the wounded, the concern now was that other Japanese forces would soon be alerted. Because so many were wounded, Sam decided they would try to get to their headquarters on the Indian border.

Desperately short of ammunition and food, they pressed on; those able were helping their wounded friends. A few times, they came across Japanese patrols and had to fight their way out. After two days' march, they reached the Indian border and made it safely to their garrison headquarters in Jhansi. Some of the men including Sam were sent to the military hospital in Delhi to recover.

For his action in the attack and helping to delay the Japanese advance, hence saving lives, Sam would later be awarded the Military Cross (MC). Many awards were made to the Chindit special forces, including four members awarded the Victoria Cross.

Chapter 13
1944

On D-DAY, 6 June 1944, the Normandy landings started. As Bob and Tommy had been aware, this was the big invasion of the continent.

The first operation that No 47 (Royal Marine) Commando was involved in was Operation Neptune. They landed on Gold Beach at 9.50 a.m. near the town of Asnelles, after a bombardment by the Royal Navy. Five of the landing craft assault carrying the Commando ashore were sunk by mines and beach obstacles with the loss of seventy-six of the four hundred and twenty men in the commando.

Bob and his section were the first ashore, but came under heavy fire from three machine gun posts as they attempted to leave the beach. It became their job to clear the way for the rest of the force and hence other forces which needed to land. Bob gave instructions to his section to open up sustained fire while he with great courage crept up on each post individually, destroying each in turn with grenades. This action saved many lives although two of his men were killed as they fought off the remaining German force. These losses delayed their advance to their primary objective: Port-en-Bessin. Leaving the beaches after noon, they fought through La Rosière and dug in around Escurès for the night, prior to their planned assault on Port-en-Bessin.

The capture of Port-en-Bessin given the codename Operation Aubery was essential for the Allies, this was to become the main port for fuel deliveries to Normandy until Cherbourg had been liberated. The assault on Port-en-Bessin began at four p.m. on 7 June, supported by naval gunfire. Bob and his men were again subjected to fierce fighting. Bob led repeated attacks on the defending Germans who put up a strong resistance. Many were killed in the action; however, the next afternoon, they captured the port as the Germans retreated. No 47 Commando now had a strength of nineteen officers and two hundred and fifty-nine other ranks, a loss of one hundred and forty-two men. The brigade was then ordered to move east of the Orne River to reinforce the 6th Airborne Division. Bob was told by his commanding officer that for his actions in helping to gain their objective, the Port-en-Bessin, he was to be awarded the Victoria Cross (VC), the highest award for gallantry.

Operation Tonga was the codename given to the airborne operation, undertaken by the British 6th Airborne Division between 5 and 7 June as part of Operation Overlord. Tommy led a section of the parachute battalion which was part of the division. By the time they boarded their aircraft, they knew with some trepidation of the invasion and the part they had to play in the D-Day landings. The paratroopers and glider-borne troops of the division landed on the eastern flank of the invasion area, near to the city of Caen, tasked with a number of objectives. The division was to capture two strategically important bridges over the Caen Canal and the Orne River which were to be used by Allied ground forces to advance once the seaborne landings had taken place. They had to destroy several other bridges to deny their use to the Germans and secure several important villages. The division was also assigned the task of assaulting and destroying the Merville Gun Battery, an artillery battery that Allied intelligence believed housed a number of heavy artillery pieces which could bombard the nearest invasion beach and possibly inflict heavy casualties on the Allied troops landing on it.

The division suffered from bad weather and poor pilot navigation, which caused many of the airborne troops to be dropped inaccurately throughout the divisional operational area, causing a number of casualties and making conducting operations much more difficult. In particular, Tommy's battalion which was assigned the task of destroying the Merville artillery battery was only able to gather up a fraction of its strength before it had to attack the battery. Tommy and his men fought hard against the heavily guarded guns. The Germans put up a strong resistance, and the depleted force suffered heavy losses. After a number of his section were killed, Tommy led his men forward in a suicidal attack that shocked the German defence and allowed the battalion to surge forward; many of the Germans were to surrender. The battery was successfully assaulted and the guns inside disabled. The division's other objectives were also achieved despite the problems encountered. They then had to create a bridgehead focused around the captured bridges until they linked up with advancing ground forces.

On 11 June, reinforcements from the holding commando in the UK brought No 47 Commando to a strength of twenty-three officers and three hundred and fifty-seven other ranks. The commando carried out patrolling, digging minefields and erecting barbed wire before being ordered to Orne bridge road to reinforce the depleted parachute division. On arrival at the Sallanelles, the area around Orne bridge Bob was to meet up with the paratroopers and his brother Tommy. As they were greeting each other with a big hug, the Germans were trying to counterattack before the heavier ground forces arrived. This meant they had to defend the area together for the first time until the artillery and tanks arrived. What a relief when the main Army arrived to push back the German assault. They had done their job separately and together; however, they were soon issued with new orders, both had to go on new operations, so fond farewells were made and a promise to see each other soon.

On 1 August, No 47 Commando moved to the Le Plein area to take over positions occupied by No 3 Commando then ordered to relieve the 49th West Riding Brigade which led to the liberation of St. Parr. They carried out a dawn attack on Dozulé which was occupied without any resistance, the Germans had withdrawn. The commando was then transported to Beuzeville where they received orders to advance towards the Seine River and cut off the retreating Germans. Bob and his men were in the thick of it again and lost more of their friends including Sergeant Jack White, a great shock to Bob who had become very close to Jack. He would now have to write to his wife and family, a great loss. The 4th Special Service Brigade moved across the Seine River in assault boats where they occupied a line along the Barentin to the Le Havre road. On 1 September, the brigade was moved up to Cany-Barville and on 2 September, occupied Fécamp which cut off the German garrison in Le Havre. The advance continued north of Dunkirk taking over positions in Ghyvelde from the Canadians. Here they remained until 26 September when they were relieved by the Black Watch.

After being relieved, they moved to Wenduine near Ostend for amphibious training on the sand dunes using LVTs (Landing Vehicle Tracked) which was a new assault troop and fire support vehicle. At the same time, the commando was brought up to strength. Bob was promoted to major and was now in command of No 47 Commando which was part of the Commando Brigade. He was aware the training had been for Operation Infatuate, the invasion of the island of Walcheren in the Dutch province of Zeeland.

Tommy with his division was returned to the UK by the Royal Navy to prepare and be brought up to strength. They were to take part in the Battle of Arnhem, which was part of Operation Market Garden. It was fought in and around the Dutch towns of Arnhem, Oosterbeek, Wolfheze and Driel and the surrounding countryside from 17–26 September 1944. Allied Airborne troops were dropped in the Netherlands to secure key bridges and towns along the Allied axis of advance. Farthest north the British 1st Airborne Division landed at Arnhem to secure bridges across the Nederrijn supported by men of the Glider Pilot Regiment and the 1st Polish Parachute Brigade. The British XXX Corps were expected to reach the British Airborne forces in two or three days.

The British Airborne forces landed some distance from their objectives and were hampered by unexpected resistance, especially from elements of the 9th and 10th Panzer Divisions. Tommy landed successfully and gathered his section together; unfortunately, this was not true for a number of the troops, many were shot down before landing. Further, some of the men were killed on crash landing the gliders. Tommy and his men were part of a small force to reach the Arnhem Road bridge while the main body of the division was halted on the outskirts of the town. Meanwhile, the XXX Corps was unable to advance north as quickly as was anticipated and they failed to relieve the airborne troops according to schedule. Tommy and his men fought fiercely against superior numbers; for four days they fought on, keeping the German force pinned down until ammunition was getting low. The small force at the bridge was overwhelmed and the rest of the division became trapped on the north side of the river. Tommy and his few remaining men headed away from the bridge and joined what remained of the division. After nine days of fighting, the shattered remains of the division were to be withdrawn in Operation Berlin. The operation was planned to save the airborne forces trapped on the north side of the river and to use small boats to ferry them across the Nederrijn at night. The surviving glider pilots led by Tommy and his section laid a white tape through the woods from the Hartenstein Hotel to the North bank of the river. Four sapper field companies of The Royal Engineer and Royal Canadian Engineer field companies were waiting with the boats. In dismal weather and under constant German machine gun, mortar and artillery fire, the boats shuttled back and forth across the wide swift river through the night. One hundred and fifty boatloads of paratroopers were recovered, saving 2500 men from the 10,095 men landed by parachute and glider at Arnhem. The Engineers lost seven killed and fourteen wounded while five were decorated for their heroic actions.

The allies had advanced through France and Belgium and although they met fierce resistance at Arnhem, the airborne forces had played a part which enabled the main armies to eventually advance towards Berlin. Tommy and his depleted section had survived and were rested at Nijmegen with the remaining division before being returned to England.

Prompted by the Normandy Landings, the Germans who had developed a V1 flying bomb, often called a doodlebug, decided to carry out attacks on the British mainland to demoralise the home front. The first attack was carried out on London. At Bethnal Green, a bridge was destroyed, six people killed and nine injured. David found himself back in command of an air group with his old 485 squadron, their task was to meet these V1s over the channel and by tipping their wings with the *Spitfire's* wings, dump them in the sea. A more dangerous task was to shoot them down. The buzzing sound of the V1's pulse jet engine was likened by some to a motor bike in bad running order. As it reached its target and dived, the sound of the propulsion unit spluttering and cutting out, followed by an eerie hush before impact, was quite terrifying, though the silence was also a warning to seek shelter. By late August, one and a half million people had left London and the rate of work production was affected. Operation Diver was put into action which included the use of anti-aircraft guns, barrage balloons, aircrafts and radar. Attacks became sustained at a rate of about a hundred a day, so David and his squadron were on constant alert to help rid the skies of this horror. They attempted to stop them before they reached the coast. To down them into the sea, radar was most important in this respect. Many still got through, although the gun batteries and barrage balloons dealt with some of them; however, of the 9,251 fired at targets in Britain, with the vast majority aimed at London, 2,515 reached the city. The casualties were terrible with 6,184 civilians killed and 17,981 injured.

David on one operation over the channel had a narrow escape, He was manoeuvring his *Spitfire* to tip over a V1 when an explosion occurred just ahead of him. A gun battery on the coast had not seen his *Spitfire* because of the bad weather and had fired and hit a V1, from which some shrapnel hit David's propeller and engine casing. David was unaware of his nearness to the coast; however, that was a good thing as he managed to glide his *Spitfire*, which fortunately was not on fire, to land in a field on the cliffs near Dover.

One of the Home Guard had seen him land. They arrived with a pickup truck and took David to their centre in a little village called West Cliffe. After a cup of tea and a nice scone, they got in touch with the Airfield at Kenley who sent a car to pick David up and take him back.

Because of the bad weather, the returning squadron landed with no knowledge of where David was, the commanding officer was very concerned and was about ready to ask for a sea search when the telephone message came in from the Home Guard. The squadron pilots and ground crew had a celebration in the local pub that night in aid of his safe return. Dot met David there and they enjoyed the evening together until a runner came from the airfield to tell them to get back quick, the radar had spotted another flight of V1 heading to London.

By the late summer, however, increasingly effective countermeasures taken against the V1 had stopped their flights and people started to return to London. Further, the Allied forces had managed to destroy their launch sites.

Unfortunately, it was not the end of the German bombing horror; a new weapon appeared — the V2. the Germans had set up launching sites around The Hague in the Netherlands. The first was launched against London on 8 September 1944 and took five minutes to fly two hundred miles from the Hague to London. The V2 explosion came without warning, it landed on Chiswick causing thirteen casualties. Intercepting the supersonic missiles in flight proved virtually impossible, other countermeasures such as bombing the launch sites were fairly ineffectual. Sustained bombardment by the V2 continued until March 1945 when at last the advancing Allies over ran the sites. In total 1,115 V2s were fired at Britain, again the vast majority were aimed at London, though about forty targeted and missed Norwich. They killed an estimated 2,754 people in London with another 6,523 injured. A further 2,917 service personnel were killed as a result of the V-weapon campaign.

The Battle of the Scheldt started on 1 November 1944 with the Special Service Brigade assigned to carry out a seaborne assault on the island of Walcheren. The Royal Marine Commandos would assault Westkapelle, Bob and his No 47 Commando landing on a small strip of sand to the right of Westkapelle, at a breach in the dyke caused by RAF bombing raids prior to the attack. The men were split up when two of the LCTs carrying them ashore beached on the Northern side of the gap instead of the Southern side. Due to the division of the force, they were late at arriving at their first objective, a radar station, having suffered the loss of thirty men and much of their radio equipment. Bob instructed his men to surround the station and when the front section attacked, they overwhelmed the defending Germans who made a retreat to find they were caught by the rest of the men and captured. Their next objective was an artillery battery which needed to be silenced, the opposition was slight until they reached the battery where the Germans were waiting. After an unsuccessful attack that evening, losing five of their troop commanders, they had to dig in for the night. The following morning, they repulsed a German attack and finally captured the artillery battery as the rest of the brigade captured the island.

At home on the farm, George never felt settled; he was eager to join his father and grandfather and enlist in the army. He proposed to Molly who he had fallen in love with and she kissed and hugged him and said "yes." At the same time, he told her he was determined to join up and help to fight the Germans before it was too late. They went into Middlesbrough and bought a ring at F. Hinds Jewellers. Molly liked a ring with a centre diamond and a smaller diamond each side.

George said, "If you like that one, it will be yours," and paid for the ring.

After that, George enlisted at the Army Enrolment Office and was told he would get a letter to report for training in a week's time. They had their lunch in Hinton's restaurant to celebrate their engagement. On their return to the farm, they had a surprise party waiting for them. June, Bill, the Land Girls twins, Milly and Cathy with their families were all there to congratulate them.

The following Friday, a letter arrived for George instructing him to report to Horfield barracks in Bristol to join the Gloucestershire Regiment for training. He was told they were short of men after the Normandy landings and a subsequent battle. So, George went off to Bristol to complete his initial training which lasted a month, before he was sent out to France with a new section of men to join the 2nd Battalion.

In March 1891, the 28th Regiment (Gloucestershire) formed part of the British expeditionary force that landed at Aboukir Bay in Egypt to oppose Napoleon's army of the East. During the Battle of Alexandria, French cavalry broke through the British lines, formed up behind the regiment and began to charge. With men still heavily engaged to the front, the order was given for the rear rank to turn about and standing thus back-to-back, the regiment held the line. To commemorate this action, the regiment began wearing a badge on the back as well as the front of the headdress, the only regiment to do this, as well as being awarded the battle honour Egypt and the Sphinx.

Chapter 14
1945

The allies were now advancing on all fronts. The Germans had been defeated at El-Alamein in North Africa, both Allied armies in Germany and Italy had the Axis forces on the run and in the Pacific, the war against Japan was being won.

George and his section arrived in Le Havre as the 2nd Battalion of the Glosters advanced into Belgium, seeing action in the bridgehead across the Turnhout-Antwerp Canal and the Netherlands where at Stampersgat, George and his section had their first taste of battle. The German resistance was fierce; however, after many days of fighting, the Germans were overcome and retreated. The battalion lost many men; among them were George's sergeant and the battalion commander. George had shown great courage in taking over when they had lost their section NCOs during the battle and was made a sergeant in the field.

The battalion pressed on and reached Nijmegen where it spent a few quiet months interrupted only by a four-day battle at Zetten in January. The battalion's last significant battle of the war came on 12 April when it assaulted across the river Ijssel at Arnhem, after which the 56th Brigade passed through to capture the town itself. Following the German surrender on 8 May, the battalion entered Germany near Osnabruck where they came across a concentration camp. The German guard had left as the Allies were approaching and many of the prisoners were wandering around aimlessly, others were dead and dying in horrid conditions, with piles of bodies everywhere, a sight which George would never forget. The battalion provided a detachment for the British guard at the Nuremberg trials and in August, it was transferred to the 5th Guards Brigade stationed in Berlin.

Between the Normandy landings on 6 June 1944 and VE Day on 8 May 1945, the battalion suffered seven hundred and eighteen casualties out of an original strength of eight hundred and forty-five men.

George was now on duty in Berlin as part of the occupation force. The remains of the battalion was relieved from its involvement in August when it returned to Britain. In September, the battalion was disbanded; however, the 1st and 2nd battalions were amalgamated. George decided to stay on as a regular soldier in the new 1st battalion. All the returning men were either demobilised or given leave to return home.

At the beginning of January, No 47 Commando carried out patrols on both banks of the Maas River and were themselves twice ambushed by German patrols doing the same. Bob and his men were able in both cases to fight back and see the Germans retreat, with some loss of men, which was always a blow to Bob. They were moved out of line to prepare for Operation Horse an assault on the island of Kapelsche Veer (Netherlands) planned for the night of 13/14 January. The assault started at one a.m. hours with No 10 Inter-Allied Commando attacking the German right flank supported by artillery from the mainland and No 47 attacking the left flank. Attacking both flanks simultaneously under heavy mortar fire caused heavy casualties. It became obvious to Bob that the objective was too heavily defended for a lightly armed commando unit to capture alone so No 47 was withdrawn. The island was eventually taken by the Canadian infantry brigade with artillery and armour support. After this assault, the No 47 was moved back to Bergan op Zoom and then on to Walcheren Island, where they took over garrison duties. While at Walcheren, Bob received a hundred reinforcements which brought No 47 almost up to full strength.

On 12 March, they moved to Beveland to relieve No 4 commando and on 16 March, they were given the task of training the 3rd Battalion of Infantry, Royal Netherlands Army formed from men in the liberated area of the Netherlands. When the war in Europe ended on 8 May, they were still in Beveland.

On 20 August, No 47 commando became the first Royal Marine Commando to have an Army troop, which Bob was not pleased with, but had to control as they moved to Oer-Erkenschwick (Germany). Here their task was the administration of displaced persons. They were moved to Warburg on 2 November and were informed they would soon be returning to the United Kingdom. By this time Bob and his men, who had fought hard with him throughout the war and lost a lot of good friends, had had enough and just wanted to get home to their families. Leaving Germany on 27 November, they arrived in Haywards Heath where they remained until they were disbanded on 31 January 1946.

Tommy and his section on their return to England became part of a reinforced 1st Airborne Division. The German Instrument of Surrender was delivered on 8 May to General Franz Bohme, the commander of all German forces stationed in Norway and the 1st Airborne Division landed near Oslo and Stavanger between 9 and 11 May. The majority of the transport aircraft carrying the division landed safely, but three planes crashed with a number of fatalities. The division encountered little of the expected German resistance. Tommy and his men were in one of the planes which was hit by shrapnel from German artillery. The word had not got through to some German units that the war was over. One of the landing wheels had been damaged so the pilot had to make a crash landing. On landing, a fire had started in the engine; however, Tommy and his men who were not hurt in the crash managed to get everyone out of the plane before it exploded. What a mess; one man dead and two with injuries. They located the rest of the division and marched into Oslo to the cheers of the inhabitants. The division acted as a police and military force during the allied occupation of Norway. Operational duties included welcoming back King Haakon VII of Norway, looking after Allied ex-prisoners of war, arresting war criminals and supervising the clearing of minefields. During its time in Norway, the division was tasked with supervising the surrender of German forces in Norway, as well as preventing the sabotage of vital military and civilian facilities. The division maintained law and order, until the arrival of Force 134, the occupation force. In August 1946, the division returned to Britain and two months later was disbanded.

During his time in Oslo, Tommy and his pals had some free time and were able to go into the city for a break. They ended up in a large bar cum dancehall.

It was there that he asked a young woman for a dance. They got on well as they had a lot in common, it turned out she was from a farming family and was called Emma Bergeson. Her home was on a farm near Hamar. She had come to work as a vet in a practice in Oslo as part of her final training. Tommy walked her home to her flat, occupied by three young women, with an agreement to meet on her day off in two days' time.

Tommy managed to borrow a Jeep and picked Emma up at around mid-morning to take her for lunch at the Grand Café. They parked the Jeep and walked past the shops, chatting in English. Emma had a good knowledge of the English, and Tommy loved her dialect. With help from Emma, they selected and enjoyed a delicious meal, in a café where it was said Munch had swapped one of his paintings for a meal.

"Come on," said Emma, "it's a good day for a walk in the park."

So they headed for one of Oslo's many parks; St Hanshaugen Park which had a lovely view of the Oslofjord. They sat on a park bench and got to know each other better, so much so they had their first kiss. Later, they ended up in the dancehall and danced together closely until Emma said she would have to get back as she was up early in the morning. They parted with a kiss and a hug and a promise to meet up again soon.

The weeks and months passed with them meeting up at least once or twice a week, each time falling more in love. On one evening, Tommy proposed to Emma, saying, "I love you very much. Will you marry me?"

She was so overcome with her love for him, she did not think of any problems. "Yes, I love you too."

Tommy had bought a ring and gave it to her. It was a perfect solitaire engagement ring and it fitted well; a good omen.

A fortnight later, Emma had finished her surgery training. She already had her veterinary degree and told Tommy she would have to return home and look for a job. Tommy arranged to go with Emma to meet her parents on the farm outside Hamar. They arrived by train and Emma's brother Peter picked them up in his car and took them to the farm. The farm was situated in a lovely valley with high ground and mountains all around. On meeting Emma's parents, they were congratulated on their engagement and Tommy was given a warm and friendly welcome, followed by an engagement party which the family had prepared for Emma's homecoming. Most of the Bergeson extended family had turned up to a noisy but happy celebration.

Emma who was a similar age to Tommy had been a champion skier before training to be a vet. The next day after the party, Emma said they should take Tommy, who had not skied before, up onto the local runs and give him some lessons. Tommy was keen to do that as an ex-athlete and a paratrooper, he was ready to have a go at any sport. The group consisting of Emma, Tommy and Emma's two brothers Peter and Eric set off to the slopes a few miles away. After a couple of lessons, Tommy had soon picked up the rudiments of the sport and was able to complete the practice slopes.

A good time was had by all, returning to the farm rather tired and ready for dinner.

That evening, Emma and Tommy had to talk about their future. After some time, it was decided that Emma would go to live with Tommy on his family farm after their marriage in Hamar. Emma's brothers would be taking over running the farm soon as Emma's parents like Tommy's were ready to retire.

Tommy had to get back to his regiment who were returning to England, so the next day before setting off back, he promised Emma he would contact her on his return, and set a date for the wedding. After a warm but sad parting, he kissed and hugged Emma and set off back to Oslo.

Although the war ended on 8 May 1945, many of the men did not return home until the following year due to the establishment of an occupation force. After his return to England and the disbanding of his No 47 Commando, Bob decided he would retire from the forces and head for home. He would receive a good Army pension as a long-serving officer. At the end of January 1946, he arrived home in Hutton Rudby to the joy of his family and the desire to have a peaceful life. Cathy could now relax a little as she had her husband home and had word that George was all right and would be home soon. The shop had been doing well even though there was still a shortage of some goods, people were still rationed and had to use ration books to buy food and clothing.

Bob asked how the children were progressing. Brian was fourteen years old and wanted to be an Engineer, Joan was sixteen years old and wanted to go in for pharmacy like her Aunt Sarah. Joan, however, had done well at athletics and was a member of the local harriers. Further, she had been picked to run for the county and had already won the junior championship at 100 and 200 metres. Both children had been helping in the shop and were glad their dad was back to take over some of the work. Cathy would also have more help and her mother would be able to relax a little as she was now at retirement age. Cathy told Bob about the street party they had when the war ended, with most of the village taking part and everyone bringing what little they could to celebrate. Bob said when Tommy and George got home, they would have a family celebration.

In June of 1946, David who had left the RAF when the war ended was married to Dorothy in the Kenly Parish church. David had been accepted to become an airline pilot and would fly from Heathrow. They had bought a house in Virginia Water so he could commute to work. Most of the family who could had arrived for the ceremony. David's family from Wales and from Yorkshire; Bob, Cathy, Sarah, Jim, June and Milly. The RAF provided a guard of honour and David's sister

Julie with Dorothy's sister Jean were bridesmaids. It was a lovely wedding and a memorable reception.

In September, George arrived home at tea-time to the relief of Cathy and Molly. The family at the shop all hugged and kissed and settled down for tea and the home cooking George had missed. Bob asked what he was doing now the war was over. George told them he enjoyed army life and would stay on as a regular soldier. After tea, Bob ran George round to the farm where another welcome awaited him from all at the farm. The Land Girls had agreed to stay on till the men returned. Sheila and Joyce had to return to South Shields in a few weeks. Molly had been waiting for her fiancé to return and after a welcome from June and Bill, she embraced George, then took him out for a walk to discuss their future. George had been given a month's leave to recover after the return from hostilities and other duties.

He said to Molly, "I am staying in the Army."

Molly was not very happy about that. A few months before, a message had come from her mother to say that her father, a commander in the Tank Regiment, had been killed in action.

George asked, "Would you be willing to be an army wife?"

Molly said, "I love you; of course, I will go where ever you go."

So, they decided to get married in the Baptist church in Hutton at the beginning of October. Now they had to make plans, so Molly would go home to see her family and George would make arrangements with his mother's help.

All was arranged for another family gathering, most of the families on both sides turned up. Molly had stayed at the farm to get ready and set off with her Uncle John, her father's brother who was a Navy officer. At the church, her sisters and George's sister Joan were the bridesmaids. George's cousin Sam was the best man and members of his platoon formed a guard of honour. What a splendid ceremony and reception they had! The reception was held in the church hall with everyone having a happy time. After the reception, George and Molly set off for a week's honeymoon in Scarborough. They would return to Bristol to live in the newly constructed married quarters built for the Gloucestershire Regiment.

Tommy arrived home in October. The family knew he was engaged to Emma. June and Bill were glad to see he was going to take over the farm and settle down. The Land Girls were leaving so Tommy was needed, although some of the younger farmhands were returning from overseas to replace the girls. All the fighting men had now returned so Bob had arranged a celebration at the farm two days after Tommy's return.

That Saturday evening, all the family were invited and the farm workers, Sarah and her family came from Stokesley and even Emily and Ted came from Wales. Everyone had brought some food or drink. Bob had managed to get a barrel of ale from the local pub. They talked about old times and discussed the future times, ate, drank, laughed and ended up round the piano singing all the well-known songs. Emily and Ted stayed at Sarah's house for the night, Cathy gave a lift home to Milly and her children. Bob, Will and George walked home together a bit worse for wear but enjoying the banter on the way.

The next week, Tommy arranged to fly back to Norway to make final wedding arrangements and to bring back Emma to meet his family. He flew into Oslo Airport from Newcastle Airport then travelled by train up to Hamar where Emma met him in the family car to take him back to the farm. Arrangements had been made for their wedding to take place at the end of November in Hamar Cathedral where the family worshiped. Emma had selected the Hotel Grand for their reception, this would enable the visitors from Britain to stay as well as the newlyweds after the wedding reception. Tommy said they would honeymoon in Wales.

Tommy and Emma made a return trip together by train to Stavanger and then by Ferry to Newcastle where Bob picked them up to take them to the farm at Hutton. The family at the farm made Emma feel at home, the twins had gone back to Shields so she was able to use the bedroom they had vacated.

June and Bill got on well with Emma and told her they would live in a bungalow being completed on the edge of the farm. Emma stayed a week before returning to Hamar. In that time, she was able to meet all of the family in Yorkshire and even had a trip to see Emily and family in Wales. It was a lovely time. Emma said to Tommy she loved him, and was happy to meet his family who were very nice people.

The wedding of Tommy and Emma took place as planned in the old Cathedral in Hamar. Tommy and most of his family had travelled over by Ferry and train, they stayed overnight at the Hotel Grand ready for the next day when they would help Tommy to get ready. Emma arrived in an open coach pulled by two white horses and was led in by her father to the alter, followed by the bridesmaids. Tommy and Bob the best man were waiting as she was led up the isle as the organ played a beautiful old Norse tune.

It was a marvellous ceremony in the great sanctuary, the bridesmaids were Emma's little cousins and Milly was maid of honour. They had the reception in the Grand which lasted well into the night with everyone having a great time. Bob's son Brian had got on very well with one of the bridesmaids, Olga who was a very pretty girl, they just seemed taken with each other. Bob had to find them in the garden and get them to come in when everyone was going home or turning in for the night. They promised to write to each other, the beginning of another relationship.

The following morning, Tommy and Emma said goodbye to their families who saw them off from the Grand. Peter had offered to drive them to the airport in Oslo. From there, they flew into Newcastle Airport where a hired car took them to their honeymoon hotel in Tenby south Wales.

Sam was sent to the British Military Hospital in Delhi where he managed to get a message to Ella and wrote home to his parents to let them know he was not seriously wounded and was recovering. At the same time, he had the sad task of sending a letter to John's parents, telling them how he had died and what a brave officer he had been leading his men into battle. Ella who was teaching would call into the hospital most evenings to see Sam, they still were very much in love. By the time Sam was able to leave the hospital, the Japanese had surrendered and Sam's regiment was stationed in Delhi, which was a good arrangement for the couple. Sam asked Ella's father again for her hand in marriage, it was granted. Major McDonald said, "I am proud to have you as my son-in-law." So, the next day, they went into the city to buy an engagement ring in the Dariba Kalan area if Delhi. In the street where the best jewellers were located, they found a beautiful platinum diamond and ruby ring which Sam bought for Ella.

Sam said, "We need to have a meal out to celebrate."

Ella told Sam, "Come back home with me, I have a surprise for you."

Back at the house on the outskirts of Delhi, an engagement party had been arranged where Ella's family and friends plus some of Sam's comrades had gathered to wish them well. It was a wonderful celebration especially when Ella produced and presented Sam with a ring, which had belonged to her grandfather. The ring was solid gold with an elephant symbol on it.

On 6 August 1945, at eight fifteen a.m., local time, the United States detonated an atomic bomb over the Japanese city of Hiroshima, calling for the Japanese to surrender. This was not forthcoming so on 9 August a second atomic bomb was dropped on the Japanese city of Nagasaki. The surrender of Imperial Japan was announced by Japanese Emperor Hirohito on 15 August and formally signed on 2 September. This was held aboard the United States Navy battleship *USS Missouri*, bringing the hostilities of World War II to a close. The role of the atomic bombings in Japan's unconditional surrender and the ethics of the two attacks causing untold misery to Japanese civilians is still debated. It should, however, be stressed that without the attacks, many more military and civilian personnel would have been lost on both sides, possibly prolonging the war by several years.

Although the war was officially over, many isolated soldiers and personnel from Japan's far-flung forces throughout Asia and the Pacific refused to surrender for months and years afterwards, some even refusing into the 1970s.

In Burma, the Japanese, who had occupied the country, assisted the formation of the Burma Independence Army. They hoped to gain support in expelling the British so that Burma could become independent. However, a puppet government was installed and many Burmese believed that the Japanese had no intention of giving them real independence. The opposition nationalist leader Aung San sided with the Allies against the Japanese and by April 1945, the Allies had driven out the Japanese.

Subsequently, negotiations began between the Burmese and British for independence. Under Japanese occupation, 170,000 to 250,000 civilians died. The efforts and sacrifice of Sam, John and many others in the Chindit force and the Indian Army had overcome the Imperial Japanese Army. Those prisoners of war who suffered and survived the cruelty of the Japanese camps and the forced labour on the railroad were free to return home. Burma would become Myanmar; a free and independent nation.

After the war, the British Empire would gradually negotiate with its colonies throughout the world and free them from British rule. This would lead to the formation of the British Commonwealth of Nations.

Chapter 15
1947

1947 was the first year of the Cold War which would last until 1991, ending with the dissolution of the Soviet Union. Most families were now adjusting to a peaceful recovery from the horrors of war; however, times were still hard. Although some goods were still rationed, things were gradually improving. The shipping lanes were free of U-boats so that imports were coming in from our colonies and America.

Tommy and Emma had taken on running the farm and were blissfully happy. Bill and June had retired to their bungalow, although they still turned up to help when necessary. Two of the farmhands who had gone to fight had been killed in action so Tommy had taken on two strong lads from the village.

Bob had taken on running the village shop with Cathy, their children had their own lives to lead; both were in their last years at school. Brian was a keen footballer and now played for the Middlesbrough junior team. Joan was still competing in Athletics. Bob, therefore, had also become a taxi driver cum manager, taking them all over the country.

Will, had no intention of leaving the village, although he was now a sergeant with the right experience to become an inspector. Bob and Will met up every Thursday evening at the village pub for a chat and a drink with some of their very old friends. They were instrumental again in seeing the council, to add the names of their friends from the village who had not returned to the war memorial.

One Sunday morning, all the village folk gathered at the memorial to unveil a plaque which had been added to the structure. It consisted of all the men and women who had been killed in battle, on the seas or on the home front in the Second World War. The bottom of the plaque read:

'In memory of all those of this village who gave their lives for our children and grandchildren, we will remember them.'

The last post was played by an old soldier and they all sang the hymn 'O Lord Our Help in Ages Past, Our Hope in Years to Come'. A sad occasion for many and a bitter memory of lost comrades for others who had survived.

George and Molly had settled in to army life in Bristol to be told the battalion was to serve in the British colony of Jamaica. They were very happy to go to the Caribbean; not many people travelled so far, so it was an exciting experience. In Kingston, their married quarters were well-maintained and it was there that their first child Harry was born. It was agreed to name him after Molly's father in memory of a brave man. Life was good in Jamaica; unfortunately, it did not last long. It was in Jamaica that, in accordance with the restructuring of the British 'Army, the regiment's two battalions swapped colours and amalgamated to form the single battalion Gloucestershire Regiment on 21 September 1948.

The winter of 1946–47 was a harsh European winter noted for its impact in the United Kingdom. It caused severe hardships in economic terms and living conditions in a country still recovering from the Second World War. There were massive disruptions of energy supply for homes, offices and factories. Animal herds froze or starved to death. People suffered from the persistent cold and many businesses shut down temporarily. Beginning on the 23 January 1947, the UK experienced several cold spells that brought large drifts of snow to the country, blocking roads and railways which caused problems transporting coal to the power stations. Stockpiles of coal at the pits and depots froze solid and could not be moved. The snow also trapped 750,000 railway wagons of coal and made roads unusable, further hampering transport. Towards the end of February, there were also fears of food shortage as supplies were cut off and vegetables were frozen into the ground. Pack ice was seen off the Belgian coast, which suspended the ferry service and ice floes were also seen off the coast of East Anglia causing a shipping hazard.

Several hundred villages were cut off, including Hutton Rudby. The farm would have been cut off from the village; however, Tommy had a tractor he could use, so with other farms in the area they managed to make the roads in the village passable so people could get to the shops, church and pubs. The farm and village folk helped each other, particularly the old were kept warm. Many had wood stocks and some coal stocks, no one went without some food and warmth. It was a hard time. When warm weather returned, the ice thawed and flooding was severe in most low-lying areas. More than 100,000 properties were affected by the flooding. The British Army and foreign agencies were required to provide humanitarian aid. The winter had severe effects on British industries, causing a loss of around ten per cent of the year's industrial production, ten to twenty per cent of cereal and potato crops and a quarter of sheep stocks. The governing Labour Party began to lose its popularity, which led them to losing many seats to the Conservative Party in the 1950 general election. That winter is also cited as a factor in the devaluation of the pound from $4.03 to $2.8 and the introduction of the Marshall Plan to rebuild war-torn Europe. In Berlin, the effects of the winter were severe with a hundred and fifty deaths from the cold and famine.

By the end of March, things in the village were almost back to some normality; traffic on road and rail were moving, allowing goods to come in, some goods not seen since before the war were gradually appearing. Some fruits like bananas and oranges and sweets which were in short supply were coming into the village shop. So, the children were seeing some things for the first time.

Sam and Ella had decided with the good wishes of Ella's family to marry in a Christian church in Delhi. Sam was now fully recovered and taking an active role in his regiment. The wedding took place without Sam's family so they promised they would have a celebration on their return to England. A wonderful time was had by all present, their honeymoon was spent in Simla in a secluded hotel. On return to Delhi, they were given accommodation in the army married quarters.

As a result of the partition of India in 1947, the formations, units, assets and indigenous personnel of the Indian Army were divided, with two-thirds of the assets being retained by the Union of India and one-third going to the new Dominion of Pakistan. Four Gurkha regiments recruited in Nepal, outside India, were transferred to the British Army forming its brigade of Gurkhas. British Army units stationed in India were returned to the United Kingdom or posted elsewhere.

The partition caused a great amount of trouble and bloodshed between the Pakistan Muslim and Indian

Hindu population. There was massive migration in both directions, causing upset and intolerance by many. Because of this friction, the two new armies of India and Pakistan fought each other in the First Kashmir War, beginning a bitter rivalry which continues into the 21 century.

Sam, Ella and a new baby boy, called John, returned to England with the McDonald family. Sam's Battalion was disbanded and he was demobbed. Major McDonald retired from the army. The McDonalds called in at Stokesley, where they were introduced to Sam's family. They then went on to Stirling where the major had a home. Sarah and Jim had told Sam they could stay with them until they were able to afford a house of their own. They were overjoyed to see Sam and his wife and son safely back and adored the baby. That evening, all the extended family from Hutton and the farm were invited round to celebrate the return of Sam and his marriage to Ella. Bob made a toast to wish the couple well.

"Thank God for your safe return, and an end to all hostilities. May your lives be happy and peaceful from now and into the future."

Sam returned to Leeds University where he finished his degree and was selected to work for Dorman Long Steel Company that later became British Steel. After a few years, he would become Chief Metallurgist at Rolls Royce, working on the first jet engines for the modern aircraft. Ella managed to get a job teaching at a local primary school.

Bob was happy to take Joan to her meetings and competitions. She had done well and had been picked to run in the Olympics, they were all proud of her achievements. Tommy was particularly interested in her progress as he had been a medal winner in 1936. He sometimes took Joan to the athletics track and acted as her coach.

The 1948 summer Olympics, officially known as the Games of the XIV Olympiad, was held in London from 29 July to 4 August. Following a twelve-year gap caused by the war, these were the first summer Olympics held since the 1936 Games in Berlin. The 1940 Olympic Games had been scheduled for Tokyo and then for Helsinki, the 1944 Games had been provisionally planned for London. In 1948, it was the second occasion that London had hosted the Olympic Games, having previously hosted them in 1908.

The event became known as the Austerity Games because of the difficult economic climate after the war. No new venues were built for the games with events taking place mainly at the Empire Stadium and the Empire Pool at Wembley Park. The athletes were housed in existing accommodation at the Wembley area instead of an Olympic Village. A record 59 nations were represented by 4,104 athletes, 3,714 men and 390 women in 19 sports disciplines. Germany and Japan were not invited to participate in the games. The Soviet Union was invited but chose not to send any athletes, sending observers instead to prepare for the 1952 Olympics.

Joan had done well at her school work and did well in her exams. Her results would get her into London University to study pharmacy. She always wanted to be a chemist like Auntie Sarah. Her life had been a routine of school, running and bed, even at weekends. She could now, however, concentrate on the preparation for the Olympics. Bob and Tommy took turns in getting her to the training ground to train with the other older athletes, she was lucky to be picked as part of the team at such a young age. The time came for Joan to join the British team down in London.

Bob and Cathy drove her down to the accommodation reserved for the Olympic teams and settled her in as it was her first time away from home on her own.

At four p.m. on 29 July 1948, the time shown on Big Ben the London games symbol, the king declared the Games open. 2,500 pigeons were set free and the Olympic flag raised to its eleven meters (35ft) flagpole at the end of the stadium. The Royal Horse Artillery sounded a 21-gun salute and the last runner in the torch relay ran a lap of the track, created with cinders from the domestic coal fires of Leicester and climbed the steps to the Olympic cauldron. After saluting the crowd of 85,000 spectators, he turned and lit the flame. The Olympic Oath was taken on behalf of all competitors, the National Anthem was sung and the massed athletes marched out of the stadium, led by Greece, tailed by Britain.

An official report concluded:

Thus were launched the Olympic Games of London, under the most happy auspices. The smooth-running ceremony, which profoundly moved not only all who saw it but also millions who were listening-in on the radio throughout the world, and the glorious weather in which it took place, combined to give birth to a spirit which was to permeate the whole of the following two weeks of thrilling and intensive sport.

Once they knew when Joan would run in her two events the 100m and 200m, most of the family who could, made their way down to London. Bob, Cathy and Brian spent a holiday down in the capital and were able to see a number of the events, including all of the races that Joan ran in. Tommy and Emma were able to see her races with Bill and June. For the finals, Sarah and Emily's families were able to be in the stadium.

Under a hot sun, Joan managed to get through her heat to the joy of the home crowd. There were three heats before the final, two of the heats were won by British women. Joan came second in her heat. In the final of the 100m. Joan was just beaten into 4 place, the silver medal was won by a British sprinter Dorothy Manley and the bronze by an Australian Shirley Strickland. The gold medal was won by one of the star performers of the Games the Dutch sprinter Fanny Blankers- Koen. Dubbed The Flying Housewife, a thirty-year-old mother of two who went on to win four gold medals in athletics.

A tremendous crowd were present when under great pressure due to the climate, Joan managed to win her heat in the 200m race, which for a young girl was a remarkable achievement. The final of the 200m was a very close thing. Half way round the track, Joan was in the lead; however, close behind her were three very experienced sprinters and again she came fourth. The gold medal was won by Fanny, the silver medal was won by another British woman Audrey Williamson and the bronze medal by Audrey Patterson from the USA.

In the decathlon, American Bob Mathias became the youngest male ever to win a gold medal at seventeen. The most individual medals were won by Veikko Huhtanen of Finland who took three golds, a silver and a bronze in men's gymnastics. The United States won the most gold and overall medals, the host nation ended up twelfth.

Tommy and the family said Joan had done extremely well for an eighteen-year-old. With the experience she had gained and her determination, Joan would go on to win medals in the 1952 Olympics. The family met up and took Joan out for the evening after her event. They had a walk by the river Thames and ended up having a lovely meal at a restaurant overlooking the Houses of Parliament.

Chapter 16
1950

In 1949, George and Molly returned to their house in Bristol after the 1st Battalion the Gloucestershire Regiment returned to the UK. They were able to travel up to Yorkshire, so that little Harry who was a lively toddler could see his grandparents on both sides. Bob and Cathy were really happy to see their eldest son and Grandson. They were able to see the rest of the family and visit Molly's family. Tommy and Emma now had a little boy Jan who was a similar age to Harry, so they spent some time at the farm to enable the boys to play together. George and Molly had spent many happy hours working on the farm, so they spent some time seeing how things were progressing. Tommy was trying to update, installing new machines and equipment to keep up with the changing advancement of agriculture. They visited Bill and June who had settled in their bungalow and were enjoying their retirement. Bill had had a heart attack, when he was rushed into hospital. It had been a worrying time for the family; however, he had recovered and was taking life easy. They had been abroad to Italy on holiday for the first time and had stayed on Lake Garda and in Venice. George and Molly with Harry said their farewells at the farm and headed back to the village shop to get ready to go back to Bristol. They had a good evening with Bob, Cathy, Brian, Joan and Cathy's mum, then the men popped round to the pub where they met up with Will and had a drink and a lot of banter. Next morning, they parted with the usual hugs and kisses and set back off to the barracks. It was quite a long journey for Harry so they stopped on the way down. George had hired a car from the company pool so they could stop when they wanted. They returned safely, tired but happy after a lovely break.

The Korean conflict escalated into warfare when the North Korean military (Korean People's Army, KPA) forces, supported by the Soviet Union and China, crossed the border and advanced into South Korea on 25 June 1950. The United Nations Security Council authorised the formation of the United Nations Command and the dispatch of forces to Korea to repel what was recognised as a North Korean invasion.

On their return to Bristol, the 1st battalion of the Gloucestershire Regiment was assigned to the 29th Independent Infantry Brigade Group and on 3 November 1950, following the outbreak of the Korean War, the battalion arrived with the brigade in Korea. George was now in charge of a section of men as part of the regiment's contribution to reinforce the United

Nations' War effort. Molly was now expecting their second child so Bob and Cathy had gone down to Bristol to take her and little Harry back to stay with them. They said the regiment was at war so they were happy to have them stay until George came back.

After the first two months of war, the South Korean Army (ROKA, Republic of Korea Army) and the US forces rapidly dispatched to Korea were on the point of defeat. As a result, they retreated to a small area behind a defensive line known as the Pusan Perimeter. In September 1950, an amphibious UN counter-offensive was launched at Incheon and cut off many KPA (Korean People's Army) troops in South Korea. Those who escaped envelopment and capture were forced back North. UN forces invaded North Korea in October 1950 and moved rapidly towards the Yalu River, the border with China. On 19 October 1950, Chinese forces of the Peoples Volunteer Army (PVA) crossed the Yalu and entered the war. The surprise Chinese intervention triggered a retreat of UN forces and Chinese forces were in South Korea by late December.

On 16 February, after UN forces launched a counter-offensive, the Glosters with support from the 225-pounders of the 45th Field Regiment RA, the mortars of 170th Heavy Mortar Battery and direct fire from 17 Centurion tanks of the 8th King's Royal Irish Hussars successfully assaulted Hill 327, south of the

River Han, for the loss of ten killed and twenty-nine wounded.

Early in April, the 29th Brigade supported by the 45th Field Regiment RA took up scattered positions on a nine-mile front in Line Kansas along the Imjin River. The 657 men of the 1st Battalion, the Glosters fighting component were spread thinly on the brigade's left flank in positions set back some 2000 yards from the river.

On 23 April, The Glosters who had resisted the onslaught of the massed Chinese divisions fell back to Hill 235. A company had now less than half its strength and with all officers killed or wounded, D company's position was now exposed and with one of its platoons badly mauled in the overnight fighting was now weakened. B and C company had been outnumbered 18:1, endured six assaults, calling in artillery on their own position to break up the last of them. Low on ammunition and having taken many casualties, the seventh assault forced them to abandon their position and just twenty survivors made it to Hill 235.

As the brigade retreated, the Glosters situation on Hill 235 made it impossible for them to join the rest of the 29th Brigade after it received the order to retreat. Attempts were made to relieve the battalion which failed and even attempts to supply the battalion by air drop were unsuccessful.

George who was now in command of a depleted D-company platoon encouraged his men to stand their ground. Several attempts were made by the Chinese to take the Hill. On one attempt, it was George who led a counter attack forcing the Chinese to retreat that saved the day. The fighting was horrific but despite their difficult situation, the Glosters held their positions on Hill 235 (to be known as Gloster Hill) throughout the 24 April and the night of the 24/25 April. In the morning of the 25th April with no artillery support and little ammunition the order was given to the company commanders to make for the British lines as best they could. Only the remains of D company under the command of Major Mike Harvey escaped successfully from Gloster Hill and reached the safety of the UN lines after several days. The rest of the battalion was taken prisoner. George with the last of his platoon managed to escape, many of the men including George were walking wounded.

The 1st Battalion had held out for three nights against overwhelming odds during the Battle of the Imjin River. The stand described by the commander of the UN forces in Korea at the time as the most outstanding example of unit bravery in modern warfare, prevented the encirclement of other UN forces for which the regiment was awarded the Presidential Unit Citation and earned the nickname The Glorious Glosters. Two men, one of them George were awarded the VC for their actions in the battle. The 29th brigade suffered 1,091 casualties, 59 soldiers of the

Gloucestershire Regiment were killed in action, based on estimates PVA casualties in the battle can be put around 10,000.

On 27 July 1953, the Korean war ended with the signing of the Korean Armistice Agreement. The Korean Demilitarized Zone was established which still divides the north and south. This agreement allowed for the return of prisoners on both sides. Of the five hundred and twenty-two soldiers of the Gloucestershire Regiment taken prisoner, a hundred and eighty were wounded and thirty-four died while in captivity.

George who had received shrapnel wounds during the battle was treated with other wounded men at the field hospital near Seoul. He with others were flown home for further treatment and convalescence. George was taken to Southmead Hospital in Bristol where his wounds were treated and he was able to get a message to Molly and his family. Bob was able to take Molly and little Harry to see George a few times during his convalescence. After a few weeks, George was well enough to leave hospital and return to the barracks. On the day he returned, he got word from Hutton that Molly had given birth to a daughter. He immediately asked for leave to go up home to see his wife and children. This was granted and he managed to borrow a car and drove up to Hutton Rudby with great haste. On his arrival, there was a warm welcome from all at the village shop and a happy family reunion. The new arrival was a pretty little baby girl they named Ann. Soon, Molly was up and about. With help from Cathy and Grandma, they arranged a christening party and Ann was dedicated in the Baptist tradition. Most of the family attended to celebrate the baby's birth.

Once the celebrations were over, George had to get back to his duties, so after sad farewells, the little family returned to Bristol. George became an officer and stayed with his regiment until his retirement.

The stress of war had taken a toll on the king's health, made worse by his heavy smoking and subsequent development of lung cancer among other ailments. His elder daughter Elizabeth, the heir presumptive, took on more royal duties as her father's health deteriorated. The king was well enough to open the Festival of Britain in May 1951.

The Festival of Britain was a national exhibition and fair that reached millions of visitors throughout the United Kingdom. Bob was able to organise a trip to London, he hired a coach from the United bus company which took thirty people from the village. Both Bob and his friend Will with their families arrived at the south bank site to wander around the Dome of Discovery, gaze at the Skylon and generally enjoy a festival of national celebration. The festival focused entirely on Britain and the Commonwealth and their achievements. The implicit goal of the festival was to give the people a feeling of successful recovery from the war's devastation, as well as promoting British science, technology, industrial design, architecture and the arts. The festival centrepiece was in London, although Festival celebrations took place in many cities around the country, it became a beacon for change that proved immensely popular with thousands of if not millions of visitors. It helped reshape British arts, crafts, designs and sports for a generation.

Bob and his party had separated into family groups on arrival with strict instructions to be back at the pickup point by six o'clock for the journey home. They took hours looking at the exhibits, taking time out for a meal at one of the new food halls; these were serve-yourself and very reasonably priced. A visit to the fair proved to be a great hit for the children and young people although the older ones were persuaded to have a go on some rides and amusements. Time passed very quickly and it was soon time to get back to the pickup point. Somehow, Joan and Brian had got separated from Bob and Cathy as it was very crowded in the fair. Bob said they will know they have to get back, so Bob and Cathy headed for the assembly area. The coach was waiting for them and gradually all the villagers arrived back tired but happy after a lovely day.

It got to six o'clock with no sign of Bob's children, then suddenly, two people could be seen running towards them. They were relieved to see them, they explained they were on a ride which had broken down and they had to wait till it was repaired.

On the way back, they all sang songs and had food and drinks, having a jolly good time. What a day it had been, they would remember it all their lives. Eventually, most would fall asleep to wake up back at the village around midnight.

On 23 September 1951, King George had his left lung removed after a malignant tumour was found. In October, after some delay due to the king's illness, Elizabeth and Philip went on a month-long tour of Canada. On 31 January 1952, despite advice from those close to him, the king went to London Airport to see Elizabeth and Philip off on their tour of Australia via Kenya. It was his last public appearance. Six days later, at seven thirty on the morning of the 6 February, he was found dead in bed at Sandringham House in Norfolk. He died in his sleep from a coronary thrombosis. His daughter flew back to Britain from Kenya as Queen Elizabeth II.

From 9 February, for two days George VI's coffin rested in St Mary Magdalene Church in Sandringham before lying in state at Westminster Hall till 11 February where over 300,000 people were able to pay their last respects. His state funeral took place on 15 February; it was a very sad time for the people of Britain and the Commonwealth. Many heads of state attended the funeral and were part of the procession from London to

Windsor. The procession went through London to Paddington Station, then continued on arrival in Windsor to St George Chapel in Windsor Castle where the funeral service took place.

Bob, Tommy and Will were able to get down to Windsor where with thousands of other people, they observed two minutes' silence in memory of the king. He was loved by many as a good man, who like many did his duty to his country. At home in the village and around the whole country, people managed to see the last journey of the king on television or in the cinema.

Joan who had had been accepted at London University to study pharmacy like her Aunty Sarah had kept up with her running. She was to be part of the British team in the 1952 Summer Olympics. Uncle Tommy who was now an Olympic official still helped Joan with her training when she was at home and her dad, Bob, was always on hand to take her to events up and down the country and sometimes abroad.

The 1952 Summer Olympics, officially known as the Games of the XV Olympiad, were an international multi-sport event held in Helsinki, Finland, from 19 July to 3 August.

Helsinki had been earlier selected to host the 1940 Summer Olympics which were cancelled due to World War II. It is the northernmost city at which a summer Olympics games had been held. These were the first games to be held in a non-Indo-European language speaking country. It was also the Olympic Games at which the greatest number of world records were broken until it was surpassed by the 2008 Summer Olympics in Beijing. The Soviet Union, the People's Republic of China, Hong Kong, Indonesia, Israel, Thailand and Saarland made their Olympic debuts in Helsinki in 1952. The United States won the most gold and overall medals.

Tommy who was familiar with travelling in Scandinavian countries accompanied Joan and the British athletics team to the games in Helsinki. The competitors' village was well-arranged. Joan and her team mates soon settled in and had an interesting time meeting up with other athletes from around the world.

The time came for Joan's events, the 100m and 200m. Bob and Cathy had made arrangements with June and Milly to help in the shop so they could get to Helsinki and see some of the events which included the women's athletics. Brian who was now training as an engineer also managed to take his holidays from work so he could be with them. Unfortunately, although Joan did well and reached the final of both her events, she came fourth in one race, and fifth in the other, her best time ever in both events. However, there was great rejoicing when she won a bronze medal in the women's 4x100m relay.

It was in the 1952 Olympics in Helsinki that Roger Bannister set a British record in the 1500 metres and finished in fourth place. This achievement strengthened his resolve to become the first athlete to finish the mile run in under four minutes. He accomplished this feat on 6 May 1954 at Iffley Road track in Oxford, with Chris Chataway and Chris Brasher providing the pacing. When the announcer, Norris McWhirter, declared the time, it was not heard for the cheers of the crowd which was 3 mins 59.4 secs. He had attained the record with minimal training, while practicing as a junior doctor.

The coronation of Elizabeth II took place on 2 June 1953 in Westminster Abbey. She acceded to the throne at the age of twenty-five upon the death of her father, George VI. The coronation was held a year after his death because of the tradition of allowing an appropriate time to pass after a monarch dies before holding such festivals. It also gave the planning committees adequate time to make preparations for the ceremony.

Among those chosen to be in the procession were ex-servicemen who had fought in the war. Bob and Tommy were invited as was George as a serving soldier. Most regiments, the Royal Navy and the Royal Airforce were represented. It was another occasion not to be missed, so a trip was arranged from the village to get people down to the capital to see the great event.

Along a route lined with sailors, soldiers and airmen and women from across the British Empire and Commonwealth, guests and officials passed in a procession before about three million spectators, gathered in the streets of London, some having camped overnight in their spot to ensure a view of the monarch. Some having access to specially built stands and scaffolding along the route. For those not present to witness the event, more than two hundred microphones were stationed along the path and in Westminster Abbey, with seven hundred and fifty commentators broadcasting descriptions in thirty-nine languages. More than twenty million viewers around the world watched the coverage.

The procession included foreign royalty and heads of state riding to Westminster Abbey in various carriages, so many that volunteers ranging from wealthy businessmen to rural landowners were required to supplement the insufficient ranks of regular footmen. The royal coaches left Buckingham Palace and moved down the Mall which was filled with flag waving and cheering crowds. The Irish State Coach carried Elizabeth the Queen Mother, who wore the circlet of her crown bearing the Kohinoor diamond. Queen Elizabeth II proceeded through London past Trafalgar square to the Abbey in the Gold State Coach.

The coronation was the first to be recorded and the ceremony lasted for some time with the final investment of the crowning. The queen was invested with the Armills (bracelets), Stole Royal, Robe Royal and the Sovereign's Orb, followed by the Queen's Ring, the Sovereign's Sceptre with Cross and the Sovereign's

Sceptre with Dove. With the first two items in her right hand and the latter in her left, Queen Elizabeth was crowned by the Archbishop of Canterbury, with the crowd chanting God save the queen three times at the exact moment St Edward's crown touched the monarch's head. The princes and peers gathered then put on their coronets and a 21-gun salute was fired from the Tower of London.

The return procession to Buckingham Palace was five miles (eight kilometres) in length, 29,000 service personnel from Britain and the Commonwealth marched with four regimental bands which took forty-five minutes to pass any given point. Behind the troops was a carriage procession led by the rulers of the British protectorates, including the Queen of Tonga, the commonwealth prime ministers, the princes and princesses of the blood royal and the Queen Mother. Preceded by the heads of the British Armed Forces on horseback, the Gold State Coach was escorted by the Yeomen of the Guard and the Household Cavalry.

The 1953 British Mount Everest expedition led by Colonel John Hunt was the ninth mountaineering expedition to attempt the first ascent of Mount Everest and the first confirmed to have succeeded when Edmund Hillary and Tenzing Norgay reached the summit on Friday, 29 May 1953. News of the expedition's success reached London in time to be released on the morning of Queen Elizabeth II's coronation.

Bob and the rest of the coach party returned home with memories they would never forget. The village was decked out with flags and bunting and like cities, towns and villages across the realm, coronation parties took place with much merriment, eating and drinking for all to indulge.

The 1956 Summer Olympics, officially known as the Games of the XVI Olympiad was an international multi-sport event that was held in Melbourne, Victoria, Australia, from 22 November to 8 December 1956, with the exception of the equestrian events, which were held in Stockholm, Sweden, in June 1956. The games were the first to be held in the Southern Hemisphere and Oceania. Several teams boycotted the games in protest of the IOC's rejection to suspend the USSR after their invasion of Hungary. The Soviet Union won the most gold and overall medals.

Tommy was again involved in organising the athletes and Joan was selected for the British team. No one else from the village managed to get to Australia; however, they all watched on television. Joan did well to reach the finals of the 100m and 200m without a medal; however, she won a silver medal in the 4x100m relay. A good way to finish her competitive running.

It was the end of one era and the beginning of a new Elizabethan era, the changes to come would breed a new generation. Life in the village would change but the character of the village would stay the same. Bob, Sarah and Emily's families continued to be close. Joan would eventually marry and take over Auntie Sarah's chemist shop in Stokesley. Brian would also marry and become a qualified engineer. Tommy and Emma would run the farm until their son took over. Bob and Cathy ran the village shop into old age, they then sold the shop and bought a bungalow.

With great pride and heartfelt thanks, we should remember those who lived and died to enable the coming generations to live in freedom and safety. Some of the past generation, our parents and grandparents can still be remembered with our love and to the younger family members they should be aware what their great and great-great grandparents did for them and their country. Truly, they were a Courageous Breed.